D0408984

1R

After the Blue Hour

After the Blue Hour

A True Fiction

JOHN RECHY

Grove Press
New York

First Grove Atlantic hardcover edition: February 2017

Published simultaneously in Canada
Printed in the United States of America

FIRST EDITION

ISBN: 978-0-8021-2589-7
eISBN: 978-0-8021-8933-2

Grove Press
an imprint of Grove Atlantic
154 West 14th Street
New York, NY 10011

Distributed by Publishers Group West

groveatlantic.com

17 18 19 20   10 9 8 7 6 5 4 3 2 1

FOR THE MEMORY OF MY MOTHER
AND FOR MICHAEL EARL SNYDER

"What is the answer?"
—Alice B. Toklas
"What is the question?"
—Gertrude Stein

Prologue

A letter came through the offices of Grove Press in New York, forwarded to me in Los Angeles, where I lived in a room in a downtown hotel on Hope Street. The letter was from a man responding in admiration to two stories I had written, recently published.

The first one, titled "Mardi Gras," had appeared in the leading literary quarterly of the time, Grove Press's *Evergreen Review*. The second, titled "The Fabulous Wedding of Miss Destiny," appeared soon afterward in what would become a famous but short-lived literary journal, *Big Table*. I had sent that second story first to *Evergreen Review*. When it was twice rejected there, I sent it, on the recommendation of one of the Grove Press editors, Don Allen, who continued to champion it, to *Big Table*, recently founded. Its editors had broken away from the *Chicago Review* when, after they had announced their intention to publish sections of William Burroughs's *Naked Lunch* and all of Allen Ginsberg's "Howl," its publications board said no to both, fearing a censorship battle.

"Mardi Gras"—which began as a letter to a friend, but was never sent—had recounted, as closely as I could remember out of the fog of hallucination, what I thought of as my season in hell, when, during the Mardi Gras carnival in New Orleans, drunk and drugged and sleepless for sex-driven nights and days, I saw leering clowns on gaudy floats tossing cheap necklaces to grasping hands that clutched and grabbed and tore them, spilling beads; and revelers crawled on littered streets, wrestling for them, bleeding for them on sidewalks; and beads fell on spattered blood like dirty tears—and I saw costumed revelers turn into angels, angels into demons, demons into clowning angels; and in a flashing moment the night split open into a deeper, darker chasm out of which soared demonic clowning angels laughing.

During the purging of Ash Wednesday, as the mourning bells of St. Louis Cathedral tolled, the withering grass of Jackson Square nearby became a battleground of bodies, of men and women besotted with liquor and pills and drugs, passed out like corpses under a frozen white sun; and I fled the hellish city.

My story of Miss Destiny was about a spectacular drag queen who longed for a white wedding and who threatened to one day "storm heaven and protest"; and it was about other queens, male hustlers, and denizens of what was then called the "sexual underground" of Los Angeles. I had lived, and was still living, among those outlaws—lost angels—living the life of vagrant hustlers who inhabited the city's downtown bars and Pershing Square, a daytime sex-hunting pickup park in the midst of the city, under rows of shrugging palm trees.

Both "Mardi Gras" and "The Fabulous Wedding of Miss Destiny" were narrated in the intimate voice of a male hustler, with discernible connections to my own life; and both would, in altered form and years later, become chapters in my first novel, *City of Night*, a book not yet even contemplated.

In bold black ink, the writer of the letter praising my stories said: "You have opened the door into a world that few people know exists, and you have revealed it with all its exuberance, which I love, and its hellishness, which you describe in one place as dominated by—I admire this very much—demonic clowning angels."

At the bottom of the letter, the writer invited me to join him for the summer on his private island, an inland island.

Escape!

My life had become entangled in Los Angeles, an entanglement of anonymous sexual encounters that only seldom extended even into morning, a situation I welcomed and guarded. Unwanted demands for affection had kept me for years running away from the large cities I had lived in since my release two years earlier from the army's 101st Airborne Infantry Division, stationed in Germany, a country still scarred by heavy bombing during the Second World War.

I wrote to the letter writer, thanking him for his praise and, noncommittally, for the invitation, anticipating more details—and airfare, not sure his invitation was legitimate. The man wrote to me again, at the address in Los Angeles I had given him. If I would like to join him on his island for the summer—this letter was brief—he would send me the airfare.

Yes, escape!

I packed the duffel bag I had kept from my army days, and I waited for the air ticket.

Two weeks passed without further contact. I unpacked my duffel bag.

The plane ticket arrived.

I left Los Angeles and said good-bye to no one, wondering whom I would be meeting and why exactly I had been invited: certainly because of the stated admiration for my writing, yes, that; and perhaps because my stories, along with the photograph of me that accompanied the first one, had aroused some fantasy or other, yes, that, too.

I was twenty-four years old, and it was 1960.

1

Even though he stood in the hot, congested airport among bodies squirming and sweating and hurrying to claim their luggage before anyone else, I determined that the imposing man, now walking toward me, was my host, a handsome man, probably in his mid-thirties, dressed casually—khaki slacks, a pale-blue shirt. He wore dark sunglasses. I had not anticipated such an attractive man, and I had imagined an older man.

"John Rechy," I introduced myself, holding out my hand.

"Paul." He took my hand firmly. "Paul Wagner. It's good to meet you."

He removed his sunglasses. His brown hair—the color of his eyes—was sun-tinted. His skin was deeply tanned. He was tall. Two open buttons on his shirt indicated a toned body, slender, like that of a swimmer. It pleased me that I, too, had left two revealing buttons open on my shirt.

I responded to a flash of competition by quickly evaluating him further: He was taller than I; but, having worked out for years, I was more muscular. Of course he had a deeper tan from being on his island; I would catch up fast. I was dressed in my own usual style—faded jeans, Levi's; a somewhat form-fitting blue denim shirt; and short-cut Wellington boots. Our different styles of dressing obviated any competition in that area. I relaxed, feeling secure.

I spotted my duffel bag and retrieved it from the luggage belt.

"Shall we get help?" he offered.

"No, of course not." I slung the duffel bag over one shoulder, as I had when I was in the army. We moved ahead, out of the airport lobby and into an ambush of ferocious heat under a white scorched sun. Even within the shade of the parking lot, the heat barely relented.

My host, Paul, opened the back of a new station wagon. I flung my duffel bag in. When he started the car, the air-conditioning rushed at us in a chilly wave.

"You're a talented writer, you must know that," he said, as if to assert quickly that I had been invited as a writer he admired, perhaps at what he might consider the inception of a promising career.

"Thank you."

"Have you had lunch?" he shifted the conversation swiftly.

"Something terrible on the plane."

He laughed—"Of course"—as we approached a roadside restaurant, and he parked in the lot beside it.

"I don't care for lunch. I haven't for a long time," I told him.

"It's an unnecessary meal," he agreed, "but maybe something cold?"

We went into the restaurant, one of those chromey coffee shops that look alike and are situated on the outskirts of cities, villages really.

A heavyset waitress led us to a booth. The way she looked at us, an unconventional couple, suggested some kind of interest or curiosity.

After we had both ordered—a dutiful sandwich, which, when it arrived soon afterward, was limp, and iced tea, since wine was served only at dinnertime—Paul said:

"My son is joining us on the island. He's on holiday from school. Sonya, my intimate friend, is already there."

A reference to his son, and the pointed reference to an "intimate friend," a woman, made me wonder whether he was indicating at the outset of our involvement that he was not homosexual (the word "gay" was still only beginning to filter into the language). If that had been his intention, his evidence was not decisive. From several experiences, I knew that such an assumption, based on marriage and having children, was not strictly warranted; I'd had several sexual connections with married men, most otherwise closeted.

Paul asked me with abrupt directness about my use of first-person narration in my writing. "Your experiences, autobiographical—all true?"

"All true? I think autobiographers are big liars."

He laughed, appreciatively, I thought. "Because ... ?"

"You can't trust what you remember, can you? Memory is too unreliable to be 'truthful.'"

"I do like that, man," he said.

Man. Surely he had used that word, so incongruous for him, to assert some affinity with what he must have considered was the language of "the streets" I had written about.

"Do you prefer fiction?" he added.

"It's more honest in its disguise ... man," I said, feeling odd to address him in that way, but deciding to accept his borrowed tone. "I think the camouflage of fiction allows more authenticity—you know, acknowledging that it *is* a 'fiction,' a terrific lie, and that you want it to be believed."

"Very good. . . . You'll like the island."

I didn't like being graded. If that continued, I'd object; and eventually I would become used to the way he changed subjects randomly, perhaps following shifting thoughts; and I would soon find out that the subject of experience, now only implied, would recur in startling questions and revelations between us, not yet, but soon.

I took out my wallet to pay for my lunch.

"No, please"—he placed his hand on mine to emphasize his insistence—"you're my guest."

Asserting control? If so, I would deal with that—I was intent on creating a level field in my relations with him, whatever they might turn out to be.

As we were about to walk out, the waitress moved hurriedly to delay our exit. She asked Paul: "You the folks on the island?"

Paul paused before responding icily, "Yes."

"The kid still there talkin' stuff?" She had rushed her words as if to make sure she would speak them.

Paul did not answer.

No doubt she was referring to his son; it was not a friendly inquiry, and Paul had pointedly ignored her.

Back in the car, Paul said: "My son, Stanty—that's his nickname; he prefers it because he hates his real name—I've told him about you, and he's excited to meet you. You'll like him. He's exceptional, and he's an expert swimmer. I warn you, he's very competitive."

That was a competition I wouldn't invite, swimming with his son or him. I had never learned to swim. "How old is Stanty?"

"Just turned fourteen."

Fourteen! From what he had said of the boy's excitement at meeting me, I had assumed someone older. What had this boy been told about me to arouse his expectations? Oh, of course, his son would want to be a writer; and if he was fourteen, then Paul would probably be older than I had thought, perhaps in his forties, the early forties. He had the exceptional good looks that some handsome men retain, appearing younger.

We drove several miles through a leafy area out of the quaint village.

"When I read your stories I felt—I know what it's like to live by one's wits. That's how I've lived my life, my adult life," he said.

I was sure he was not referring to the kind of hustling that I knew, street and bar hustling that I preferred because of the blunt directness I considered honest. Although he had relegated that association to his "adult life," I chose not to respond with any welcome of kinship, which I seldom, if ever, felt or courted.

He parked in a cleared space at the edge of a sprawling lake. We walked out of the car onto powdery dirt, like beach sand. Trees lined the inland shore; they were vivid green, not scorched by the sun. There was not the slightest rustling of their leaves, not a whisper of a breeze. Two rowboats were secured to a post next to two motorboats. The water, pristine, almost crystalline, was so calm, the day so traumatized with heat, that the boats made no movement on the lake.

"Island! Island!"

He had shouted those two words—startling me—as he looked out to the distance.

"Island! Island!" came a distant answer from the lake.

"Island . . . ?"

"That's what Stanty first said," he laughed, "when I brought him here the first time. He said it was as if we were entering a world that was his and mine. We signal to each other that way."

I grabbed my duffel bag before he could and shoved it onto a motorboat.

"Just out of the army?" he asked me, nodding toward the duffel bag as we boarded the boat.

"A couple of years ago," I said. "I'm glad to be out."

The motorboat moved smoothly along the water, stirring it up in double fans of foam. The island we were approaching was lush shades of green, clusters of trees, a green oasis. The house on it was large, split into two wings jutting out on the lake like arms welcoming, or clasping.

My eyes wandered away, gauging the breadth of the lake. A distance apart was another island. It looked abandoned. The sun cast only gray patches on it as if avoiding it.

"That island," Paul said over the sound of the motorboat, which he was guiding expertly, "is vacant."

"For sale?" I asked. Even from afar, it looked neglected, left to die.

"Difficult to sell," Paul said. "Its background—"

"What happened there?"

"Nothing," he said. But still gazing in its direction, and quietly as if speaking out his thoughts, and—this occurred to me—as if quoting memorized words, he said: "What happens to evil when its flames are snuffed? Does it wait to spring out?"

He looked away from the distant island. He laughed. His tone turned ironic, parodying his own words: "That lofty shit, man—it stuck with me from a crazy book I was reading. No, I'm not a religious crank, not religious at all."

"I'm relieved," I said, and I was: I had thought perhaps his invitation had been sent with a desire to "purge" me of imagined sins gleaned from my stories. I was glad to accept his explanation, much more consistent with the man I was with. I could agree with his disdain for religion. Born into a Catholic family, I had long since abandoned any religious connection.

There was this, too, that I was ready to welcome: For long stretches of time, on the streets, I had pretended that I was not smart, only street-smart; that was widely preferred by those who picked up a type of hustler that I represented, which included an emphatic, even strained, masculinity. I had played that role, while often missing the part of myself that was smart, that welcomed intelligent conversation. This brief interlude with Paul had already released me from that restrictive role.

I stared at the neighboring island, now even more shadowed as the setting sun withdrew more light. Yet even in its drabness, it seemed dormant, as if waiting for a new tenant to resurrect it, or entirely destroy it.

"You come here every summer?"

"Yes. I come here with Stanty, and now Sonya, and, now, you."

We reached the dock. I got out and heaved my duffel bag over my shoulder while he fixed the boat in place. He smiled, a friendly smile. "Welcome to the island," he said.

Island, island! I thought. That exclamation remained echoing, curious despite Paul's explanation. It sounded more like the urgent exclamation of a drowning man.

2

As we walked toward the house, the green thickness of trees parted onto a rolling lawn of grass, a lawn on which—

I stopped, startled by the spectacle.

—a lawn on which had been arranged several sculptures. At a glance, I took in six—separated from each other so that each was stark, isolated, tall—perhaps four feet high; dark iron figures, corrugated, with extremely thin erect bodies, grotesque yet elegant, solemn.

Paul identified the artist in an ordinary tone. "They've been on loan to the museum. I take them out when I'm here."

I still had not moved. The statues, incongruous on the lawn, were like somber sentinels. I had recognized the name of the artist, a famous one in modern art.

A boy, a young man, came running to meet us—no, not running, but sauntering like someone attempting, not entirely successfully, to ration a display of anticipation. He stood before us as if to assure himself that he had our full attention. He was a good-looking boy, already resembling his father. His hair, longish, streaked blond by the sun, was still wet—like his trunks; probably he had been swimming when Paul called out their signal from the shore. His body—with dots of water glistening on his deep tan—already suggested that of a swimmer, like his father's. I decided that he was too young to arouse my sense of competition.

"My son," Paul identified. "Stanty, this is John Rechy." He rubbed the boy's head playfully.

The boy dodged the gesture. "I'm too grown-up for that, Father," he protested, although he did not entirely pull away from the gesture of affection and then tilted his head to allow it. Resuming a commanding pose, and with rigid formality, he held out his hand for me to take.

"Hello, John Rechy," he said. "I'm Stanty."

"Stanty," I said, and reached for his hand, which he quickly withdrew, laughing—suddenly a boy playing a familiar trick. But quickly he was an adult again, firmly shaking my hand. "Actually—can you believe this?—the real name they gave me is—" He looked up at his father with exaggerated accusation, waiting for him to supply the banished name.

"Constantine," Paul announced.

"Can you believe it?" Stanty said, shaking his head wildly in agitation, then delightedly sprinkling dots of water—a playful, exuberant kid again.

"It's an elegant name—Constantine," I said.

"You see?" Paul nudged him.

"It's ugly," the boy dismissed. "Please call me Stanty," he addressed me as we moved up the slight slope of the grounds toward the house.

His note of command added to the annoyance I was beginning to feel that Paul was allowing him to take over—although the feeling of annoyance lessened as he turned to me with the ingratiating smile of a boy welcoming a new friendship.

"Did you ever have another name, John Rechy?" he startled me by asking, drawing my attention away from the blunt display of statuary, an exorbitant exhibition of a collector's possessions.

"John Rechy, did you ever—?" Stanty seemed annoyed that he had to repeat his question. Now he was irritating me by linking my names for whatever purpose of his own.

"Yes, my real name is Juan," I told him, thinking that would please him.

"If you will forgive my asking: Why did you change it?"

He seemed to flex before us, straining to show off budding muscles. I laughed unintentionally.

Paul looked quickly at his son.

"You laughed at me," the boy said to me in a small voice, as if he had been profoundly wounded. He turned to Paul: "Father?" he asked, as if seeking guidance.

"I'm sure he wasn't laughing at you," Paul told him.

"Then at who—whom?"

"At myself, Stanty." I saw an opportunity to adjust the matter. "I laughed at the memory of how my own name was changed. See"—my backing off was working—"I didn't change my name"—the boy was looking at me with anticipation—"a grammar-school teacher couldn't pronounce it—it's Spanish. Mexican," I clarified. "She changed it to John." Actually Johnny, though I didn't tell him. And that was true.

The boy walked a few feet ahead. Stopping before us so that we had to halt facing him, he said, "Why didn't you change it back, then? Was it because you don't look like a Mexican and didn't want to be?"

He had struck meanly. Paul, who remained silent, seemed to be waiting with curiosity for what might follow between me and the boy.

As I remained quiet, gauging the insult, Paul finally interceded: "Stanty, I think our guest might misinterpret your question."

"Oh, then, it's easy to apologize. I'm sorry." The boy turned to me, smiling broadly: "I didn't mean an insult. There were two Spanish boys—Mexican boys—in my school, and they kept saying they were Spanish. I didn't understand why, because they were very smart, like you."

I had prepared a harsh answer to his rude question, but I abandoned it because of Paul's cautioning reaction toward Stanty—even if late, and mellow—and because of the boy's apology and unabashed compliment.

But without knowing it, although perhaps suspecting it, he had questioned me in a disturbing way that echoed a judgement. In El Paso, Texas, where I was born, people of Mexican descent would sometimes claim to be "Spanish," attempting to overcome pervasive, and still at times lingering, prejudice against Mexicans. My father was born in Mexico of Scottish descent, and I had inherited a fair complexion and "Anglo" features, especially since my mother, who was Mexican, was also fair.

Despite his apology, I felt the need to alert this boy—and to do so in front of his father—that I would not accept his rude comportment, to check it. Remembering her tone of displeasure, I said: "A waitress in town asked about you."

"That gossipy old strumpet?" Stanty said angrily.

"Strumpet?"

"That's an old English word for a whore," he said.

I succeeded in withholding my laughter.

As if to halt the subject, he took my hand and Paul's and led us—this time running and unsuccessfully coaxing us to run—to the house, shifting again, whooping joyously. "Sonya!

Sonya!" he called out to a woman standing at the main entrance
to the house.

Her astonishing figure looked naked, only a burnished silhouette in the sunset. When we approached her more closely—
Stanty still holding our hands and leading us ahead—I saw
that she was wearing a pale saffron-colored bathing suit and a
wide hat, the same color, a beach hat. Under it, her dark, long
hair fell to her shoulders. She wore large round glittery silver
earrings. Because of the hat shading her face, I could not make
out her features, though I saw more of her sensational body.

"Sonya, this is John Rechy," Paul introduced me.

"Hello, John," Sonya said, with a slight French accent.

Stanty said, "His real name is Juan, isn't it?"

I had not answered the woman; so it was easy to ignore
him, although he tilted his head, waiting.

"Hello, Sonya," I said. Stanty's mother? No, too young,
in her mid-twenties.

"Sonya isn't my mother," Stanty clarified my first thought.
"I bet that's what you were wondering. She's my father's mistress."

Now that she had moved out of the shadows, I could
gauge her expression: not the slightest frown at Stanty's blunt
designation of her. Instead, she reached out to touch his bare
shoulder, a gentle acknowledgement of his presence.

Laughing at Stanty's boldness, Paul leaned down and again
mussed the boy's hair.

This time the boy easily accepted the gesture. He rushed
on, addressing me, then Paul: "My mother will be here soon.
Won't she, Father?"

Paul nodded. "I believe so."

"Which one, Father?" Stanty asked. "Elizabeth or Corina?"

Which mother? Certainly that hadn't been what he meant.

"Perhaps both of them," Paul answered, easily conversational.

One Paul's ex-wife, another the current one? Whatever relationships were involved—and with Sonya?—those three women would be bound by their closeness to Paul. What would be my place in all this? What role was I expected to play? My conjectures about Paul's motives for inviting me shifted into new questions. I marveled at his smooth tone throughout what might have been an uncomfortable matter.

"Isn't Sonya beautiful?" Stanty asked me.

As if to confirm the boy's words, Sonya removed her hat and shook her hair free—moist from swimming.

"Yes, she is," I said. "Very beautiful." And she was. Her face matched the beauty of her body. She was somewhat dark-skinned, or perhaps only deeply tanned. Her breasts, exposed against the tautness of her bathing suit, formed perfect crescents. Her eyes were so dark they appeared black, truly black. She had full lips, scarlet with lipstick, the only makeup that I could detect.

Paul said to her, "Did you hear that, beauty? Our guest is already in your clutches."

"But he's—" Stanty pushed himself into the conversation, then stopped, about to say what?

"I'm glad you're here, John. We'll be friends," Sonya said, as if sensing an uncomfortable potential in what Stanty was about to say.

She took my hand and resumed guiding me into the house.

"I am, too, John Rechy." Stanty clutched her free hand. "I'm glad, too, and *we'll* be friends."

There was urgency in his declamation. "I think we are, aren't we?" I said.

3

The house, the inside as well as the outside, had an elegant rustic quality. Large beams spanned the ceiling. Spare furnishings, wood and leather, provided a spacious appearance. Its two wings extended outward. The main room parted into a large dining room, which was already set with white plates, wineglasses. Two candles, unlit, stood poised in silver holders. Balustered steps at one side of the room led to a lower floor. A wide sliding glass door, somewhat incongruous in the rustic setting, opened onto a spanning deck that faced the lake, silver under the light of the ending day.

As Sonya and Stanty moved away, together, to prepare for dinner—"I'll accompany Sonya to her room," Stanty said in his alternating quaint way—Paul led me to a bedroom in the wing opposite the one where Sonya and Stanty had gone.

The bedroom—my bedroom—like the rest of the house, was sparsely furnished, the bed, a desk, a bookshelf, two lamps, all suggesting an expensive quality. A large window framed the lake—I could hear the murmuring of the water.

"I've brought your duffel bag in," Paul said. "If you need anything, my room is next to yours."

"I'm sure everything's fine," I responded, and thought: with one exception, a large painting.

It hung on a wall over the desk, a painting of dizzying colors—an excellent reproduction—scrambled dots, writhing streaks twisting and turning within the frame, like mobiles, a painting I was familiar with and didn't like.

"I'll see you at dinner," Paul said, and added what had become his word of camaraderie: "... man."

I thanked him ... man. As he walked out, I felt again a pang of competition. No doubt about it, he was a handsome man, and the fact that his mistress was so beautiful added to that impression, especially because he had reacted to her as if she was on exhibition.

I looked out the window. The deserted island was visible from here, an outline, blurred by a layer of gray clouds that dissipated a short distance from it into the darkening sky.

I did not expect that anyone would dress for dinner. The casualness of Paul's clothes—and the others'—suggested informality. I had brought few clothes with me, only what fitted, crushed, in my duffel bag; that was what I did on leaving a city—what didn't fit, I left behind. I had kept a pair of khaki pants and a shirt from my time in the army. On the army shirt I had left the single stripe sewn onto one shoulder; it indicated that I had left the army as a private first class, the second-lowest rank. I had never been promoted, because of minor infractions—reading in formation (Freud on dreams), smoking in ranks, late for reveille. I had also kept a pair of olive-green fatigue pants. To the duffel bag, I had added two pairs of Levi's, socks, jockey shorts, T-shirts, two pairs of bathing trunks, and a white shirt (wrapped carefully in a plastic bag) in case I needed one.

After showering—the cool water turned into steamy heat on my skin when I left the shower—I put on the khaki pants and the shirt with one stripe. Although they were wrinkled, the hot moisture from the lake might press them. I checked myself in the long mirror against the bathroom door. Stiff. I rolled up the shirtsleeves and opened two buttons, a defiant distortion of the army's rigorous code of dress.

(Only minutes before being discharged from the army, still on the campgrounds in Kentucky, I readjust the uniform, twisting the tie over an open button, cocking the required cap. I feel free. I'm stopped by a military policeman in a jeep.

("Hey, soldier, I can court-martial you for being out of uniform. Are you drunk?"

("No, sir." So near to my release—despising having to say that and do this—I adjust the uniform.

(The pacified MP drives away in a snarl of dust.

(I assert my freedom again, distort the fucken uniform.)

I glanced about the room.

On top of the bookshelf lay a book, André Gide's *The Counterfeiters*. Arrogant of Paul to suggest what I might want to read out of several other books that filled the shelves. Still, this book, which I had read and admired, added to the sense of welcome departure from my street life. Maybe Paul intended us to discuss that book.

I walked over to the print on the wall.

It was not a print. It was the famous painting.

Just as I had anticipated, no one had dressed for dinner. Sonya wore a pale-blue, almost diaphanous dress that embraced the curves of her body. Paul was also in khakis, and a tan shirt open in a long V—ironically, we were similarly dressed. Stanty wore baggy shorts and a sleeveless T-shirt.

Now lit, the candles on the table cast a soft, benign glow. It was not, nor would it be in the days that would follow, a fussy dinner—I wondered who had prepared it—cold roast meats, a crisp cool salad, French bread, fresh vegetables, fruit and cheese, and expensive wine. There was also an incongruous plate with small jars of various flavors of jam, clearly—and this amused me—for Stanty, who slathered his bread generously with one or another at every bite.

The conversation was ordinary, mostly casual inquiries about my trip here from Los Angeles. Then it turned to the exceptional heat. Paul said he would drive into the village for electric fans. "The heat started last night," he explained, "and it hasn't relented. That's unusual because of the lake."

Stanty turned to me: "We'll go swimming; the water is real—very—cool."

I assumed he was still trying to make up for his earlier remark. Although I nodded, of course I would not go; but I was embarrassed to say I didn't know how to swim.

"The water was only a bit warm today, wonderful," Sonya said.

"Just for you, beauty, just for you," Paul said and leaned over to kiss her, a long kiss.

I heard a motorboat approaching, distant, closer, and then the sound became muffled. It stopped, near. No one else seemed to heed it, a familiar sound at this time of the evening, I supposed. After a few minutes, a gaunt man and a gaunt woman—like twin shadows—entered the house, soundlessly carrying the statues in from the garden. After they had brought

all of them in, and lined them up, the silent couple, each with
a single statue, one by one, and with extreme care, descended
the stairway into the depths of the house. After a short time,
the two gray figures emerged. I had turned away from them to
answer some question; and when I looked back, the two had
left as soundlessly as they had appeared, as if they had vanished.
Servants, of course. It occurred to me that they resembled the
statues they had secured downstairs.

That added to a momentary sense of something unreal
in this house that floated on a private island miles away from
the nearest village.

4

After dinner we sat on the deck in cushioned wooden chairs whose backs could be lowered like those on beach chairs. The deck extended partially over the lake, at the edge of which the sun had left behind hints of the blue radiance soon to come.

We lingered, drinking a cool wine Paul had just opened, different from the one that had accompanied dinner. Evening had brought no respite from the heat. Paul had served the wine— carefully less for Stanty, a fact he surprisingly accepted; he sat cross-legged on the floor next to the chair Sonya had occupied.

Standing, I stared out toward the horizon, Sonya next to me. All that remained of the sunlight was a golden arc already fading as a thin veil of darkness glided over it. A deep blue glow loomed over the water.

"I never tire of the sunset on the lake," Sonya said, "especially at its last moments."

"It's the blue hour," I told her.

"How beautiful. The blue hour. What is that, John?" she asked.

"It's not an hour at all, just a few seconds of blue light between dusk and night," I said. It was a light I cherished. On

the beach in Santa Monica, I would linger on the sand waiting for the start of sunset, an orange spill over the horizon,
soon veiled by a blue darkening light. Gulls would fly onto the
beach, gathering at the shoreline, beaks pointed at the water.
Often, lithe bodies came to perform a dance of tai chi at the
edge of the ocean. Their graceful motions seemed to me to
acknowledge and confront the night. "Some people claim that's
when everything reveals itself as it is, Sonya." I was cherishing
her rapt attention. "They say everything is both clearest and
most obscure—a light that challenges perception, revealing
and hiding."

"I like that," Sonya said, "revealing and hiding."

Stanty stood up, pressing himself sideways against Sonya,
hugging her, trying to distance her from me, I suspected. Sonya
laughed softly at his tight embrace, easing him away fondly.

"Dark and light at the same time!" Stanty said, looking
at me. "That's not possible, is it, Sonya?"

Sonya said, "It is. Look!" She pointed across the lake. The
blue cast was almost gone. "It's gone," she said wistfully. "Such
mysterious ambiguity."

Onto the deck, the soft hypnotic rhythm of Milhaud's *La
Creation du Monde* wafted through hidden speakers from the
lower level of the house. I was amused to notice that Stanty,
back on the floor and next to Sonya, now reclining in her
chair, had carried away with him from the table the plate
of assorted jams, taking a spoonful every so often, a gesture
so childish that I wondered how he reconciled it with his
posture of maturity.

Gathering clouds and a frail moon cast a misty shroud over the forsaken, distant island.

I sat next to Sonya on the other side of Stanty. Facing us, reclining on his chair, Paul shifted into another subject—I would discover later that he might also shift from one subject to another, abandon it, and then resume it exactly where he had ended it, even if on the next day. "And so, man, you write in intimate first person about your own experiences—in order to lie, as you claim?"

It did please me that he had retained that from our brief conversation earlier today. Today! I had not been here a full day, and yet I felt I had been pulled into this fantastic group. "Yeah," I answered Paul, not yet able easily to address him as "man," "because memory writes its own narrative."

"All lies, then." Often, when he asked a question, it became not so much an inquiry as a statement of his own, or a challenge.

"Only if I claimed they were the absolute truth. The claim of truth is the lie."

Paul said, "Good, that's good, man."

I considered protesting his grading me. I decided not to, not this first night.

"If you wrote about us, what would you say?" Sonya asked, leaning back, her tanned legs emerging out of the hem of her dress. Each time I looked at her, I was struck by her beauty, rare, extreme beauty, her own.

I welcomed her question, so direct and unambiguous. I sensed the beginning of unique camaraderie. "I would describe *you*," I said, "as a most beautiful woman." When I get to know an exceptional woman like her, I think that if I were not homosexual, she would be a woman I would love.

Sonya laughed. Sensual laughter consistent with her presentation.

"But how else would anybody describe you, beauty?" Paul said, and to me: "And if you ever write your autobiography, will you acknowledge that it, too, is a lie?"

"I would call it 'Autobiography: A Novel.' I lost my faith in biographies, and, later, much more, in autobiographies—when I was writing a paper in school about Marie Antoinette."

Stanty laughed. "About the guillotined queen? I thought you were raised poor, John Rechy."

He had read the brief biography that had accompanied my published stories. "Yeah, I was, but I was still writing about the tragic queen."

"That's"—Stanty paused as if for the exact big word—"incongruous."

In a strict sense it was. My interest was aroused when I was a kid and I saw a movie about the doomed queen. During "revival week" one movie theater showed only old movies and great serials, different ones every day. I saw them all, cutting grammar-school classes and sneaking in through a back door I secretly kept unlatched. Like the books I read hungrily, sometimes two or three at once, shifting from one to another, movies were my escape from my father's violence amid my mother's gentle love.

"You saw old movies in El Paso? In Texas?"

I ignored Paul's needling. "Yeah, at the Texas Grand Movie Theater . . . man." That would placate him.

"And? About the 'tragic queen'?" Paul goaded me.

"I did research, especially in Stefan Zweig's biography. There was a passage that said that on their wedding night the draperie enclosing the royal bed didn't sway all night. How the hell could he claim that was true?"

"Only suggesting what really didn't go on," Paul said.

"But with such authority," I said. "He was a good liar, he was convincing."

Sonya said, "I cried when I saw that old film about her. I saw it again, hoping that by some miracle she would be saved this time."

Paul said, "You thought the ending of a film would change to suit your sentimental expectations, beauty?"

"I was only a child," she said.

I resented Paul's chastising her. I wished that earlier I had described her as beautiful and smart. For now I defended her. "I, too, wished she had been saved."

"She drowned," Stanty said.

He was staring in the direction of the vacant island now absorbed in the distance by night.

"She didn't drown," I corrected him, although he knew that—he was planning something. "She was killed."

Paul's stare was steady on his son "Why do you say that, Stanty? You know that she—"

"Because if they chopped off her head"—Stanty aimed at me—"her head fell into a bucket. and that's where she drowned." As if the image he had gleefully conjured did not satisfy him, he rushed more words: "She drowned in a bucket of her own blood." He dipped into the jar of jam he still held, shiny, red, like coagulated blood, and he ate a large spoonful. "Her head continued to breathe, and she drowned."

"How monstrous," Sonya said.

I stopped the urge to laugh at his grotesque exaggeration. I didn't want to halt the conversation he had interrupted.

Paul astonished me by saying, easily, lazily drawling: "You see, man, Stanty found the truth in lies."

Paul's absurd rebuttal annoyed me. I had the impression that he and Stanty were indulging in a game of their own.

Lunging back into our conversation, Paul asked me about the novel that had been announced with the excerpts that had led him to invite me here, a novel I had not started but had chosen to claim existed in part, in order to secure publication of my two stories. "It'll be about the people I met on the streets, hustlers, queens," I told him, "but I'll have to overcome a feeling that I'm invading their lives."

"Invading!" Paul reacted. "Man, a writer must be a thief of lives."

"Maybe . . . man." That was all I could think of to counter him.

"In a world of clamoring clowns and malignant angels, you feel hesitant as a writer?" he asked.

"Only lies?" Sonya said. "Is it really only lies?"

I said what I knew she wanted—perhaps needed—to hear. "No, it isn't all lies."

She touched my hand, as if in gratitude. "Paul," she said, "some more music before I go to bed?"

Did he sleep with her, or did he only have sex with her?

Paul turned up the volume on a control panel on the wall, playing the same record again.

"Lovely," Sonya said. "Do you like Milhaud?" she asked me.

"I do, yes," I said, "especially *The Creation of the World.*" As I followed Stanty's gaze toward the vacated island on the lake, this occurred to me: His gory interpretation of the queen's death by drowning—was it possible that what had been on his mind was whatever had occurred on that island? I searched for the distant island from where I sat; but the night had turned so dark that it was invisible, melded into darkness. No—wait.

A forlorn house seemed to emerge within my vision, a darker shadow within the hot black night.

Sonya stood up to retire. Stanty rose with her. She went to Paul to kiss him, a kiss that lasted to the point that I looked away from Paul's implied exhibitionism.

When, a few moments later, Sonya walked past me, she kissed me lightly on the cheek. "Thank you," she whispered.

Stanty hugged Paul and kissed him on the cheek. "Good night, Father," he said.

That manifestation of ordinary affection jarred me into realizing this was the same boy who had just spun a violent story about a beheading. He was walking toward me as if about to hug me, perhaps defiantly to kiss me, to test my reaction before Paul and Sonya. I pulled back.

"You didn't think I was going to kiss you, did you? Or did you jerk away from me because of what you write about?"

"Stanty—" Sonya cautioned.

"And what would that be, Stanty?" Paul said.

I tried to hide my anger, both at Stanty and at Paul for encouraging him. "Yes, Stanty, what do you mean?" I asked.

"You know," he said. "In my school there are two boys who—oh, you know; they're quee—"

I blocked his word: "Homosexuals?" I finished for him.

"Yes," he said. "Homosexuals, that's what I meant."

He was a boy, a kid, a reckless kid, the son of my host; and I was about to engage him. But I had to react, to check him, here in front of Paul—a message to both son and father. "You seem to have two of everyone in your school," I said. "Two Mexicans, two homosexuals, two— What next? Two Constantines?"

Paul and Sonya both laughed with me.

Stanty winced. "I——" he stammered.

"That's enough," Paul finally cautioned.

Stanty assumed his commander's pose. He wasn't through.
He waited.

There occurred then the terrible stasis in time when the
expectation of something disturbing, physical or verbal, holds
all in abeyance, and all action is halted.

Into the mesmerized silence, Stanty laughed, a kid's
delighted laughter approving a move in a game. "I was just
joshing with you," he told me,

"I knew that," I said, smiling back to dismiss his remark.
The utter strangeness of this event struck me, the abrupt shifts
in conversation—and, now, everything seemed placid as if there
had been no hint of confrontation: Paul stretching, yawning
lazily; Sonya smiling at Stanty as they moved along. It was as if
a play had ended, and in the background the cadenced music
of Milhaud was fading and there was a sense of surface in the
silence, a benign surface over an undercurrent, deep down in
the lake, a current that was gathering pressure.

5

"Good night, man."

"Good night, Paul."

Paul walked out after having led me to my room. I assumed he would now join Sonya.

I took another cold shower, which cooled me briefly.

In my jockeys, I went to the window. An odd feeling of anticipation, or, more, perhaps something like anxiety, made me stare into the heated night. The vacated island had drowned in darkness.

I roamed over to the shelf with the books Paul might have chosen for me. I pulled out Camus's *The Myth of Sisyphus*. It had exhilarated me when I was a freshman in college, on a scholarship—the only way I could afford it, and for only two years even then—not caring about a degree, taking only courses in literature and a course in film, bravely supported and taught in the small college by a Harvard professor who had sought El Paso's tepid weather to nurture his diminishing life. Right after the two years in college, I volunteered to be drafted into the army to obviate the inevitable conscription. From Camus's book, I had copied the following: "The only

way to deal with an unfree world is to become so absolutely
free that your act of existence is an act of rebellion." That
still mattered, but would the book excite me now? Better
not risk the danger of years-ago impressions recalled. I put it
back. *Tristram Shandy*—I leafed through it, evoking its terrific
inventions, especially the creation of an impatient reader as
a character.

It was too hot to read. My eyes kept wandering to the
disturbing painting on the wall—the dots and lines seemed
to move and swirl. I would have covered it with a towel, but
the towel I had used was moist. I lay in bed, which, for a few
moments, was notably cool.

If it continued, I would have to deal with the fact of
Stanty's rudeness. Playful rudeness perhaps, and there were
his ready apologies, and Paul had finally checked him. I could
leave; Paul had sent return fare to Los Angeles. But I didn't
want to leave.

I had fled Los Angeles to break all contacts, feeling a
need for a respite, a new life—or, rather, a return to an earlier
life of reading hungrily, a life which I am already finding
here in conversations with Paul. I don't know why—after
leaving the army, asserting my solitary existence even within
the imposed camaraderie among soldiers—no, I don't know
why I turned to vagrant wandering and hustling, pretending
to be only street-smart like other exiles living from day to
day on the precipice of cities, exiles I joined and became one
of. Nor do I know why I abandoned my former isolation;
perhaps—this must be it—I wanted to slaughter as violently
as I could a sense of rotting innocence entrenched, self-
imposed, during which I lived mostly through books and

movies to escape the reality of a harsh existence, a menacing
father not tempered even by the gentleness and wounded
love of my mother.

Paul.

Paul, a fascinating man whose purpose in inviting me
here was still, despite my conjectures, an enigma—and, too, I
would stay because I welcomed Sonya's suggestion of a unique
friendship. Yes, I would stay here for now, yes, on this island.

Lulled by the slapping of the water against this side of
the house, I fell asleep, only to be wakened—I thought no
more than an hour had passed—by the sound of footsteps
approaching along the hallway; that would be Paul returning to his room next to mine. The soft footsteps—bare feet,
or slippers—paused outside my door. Was I still asleep? No,
I was wide awake. Definitely someone had stopped outside
my door.

Sitting up, I listened. I was sure someone was standing
there. Waiting for what? The footsteps had faded, perhaps
smothered by the sound of lapping water outside. Of course,
it was Paul on his way to his bedroom and pausing to see
whether I was asleep, perhaps to say good night again. It would
not surprise me to know, as I had suspected, that he did not
spend the whole night with Sonya. The footsteps resumed,
but now they were retreating, not proceeding to where Paul's
room was, but going away from it—this was a strong impression. Then who had stopped outside my room? Sonya?—to
tell me what? Stanty, playing another silly game? Sleepily, I
reassured myself. Paul had forgotten something and had gone
back to retrieve it. I fell asleep concentrating on the sound of
the water outside—but once again I was wakened.

There was now the sound of the motorboat heading to the house, at first distantly whirling, and then quiet, subdued, as if allowed to coast, becoming invisible on the water.

In the morning, all my disturbing impressions faded. Not dreams, no—I had definitely been awake—just the accretion of impressions gathered during the brief time I had been here, all blending into the ambiguous sounds and sights of the night. I walked to the window. Despite the bright morning glare—and the unbudging heat—the neighboring island was encased in heavy fog that seemed to have gathered only there.

I was not surprised to learn that breakfast was an individual event. Every morning there was, and would be with few variations, imported coffee, freshly ground—dark, strong, very strong—fruit or juice, croissants, assorted pastries, French bread. All was prepared, I assumed, by the soundless gray couple.

After I had coffee and a French roll, I encountered Paul coming in from outside to seek me out. He offered to show me the library.

He was wearing trunks and a tank top. I had already determined correctly that the form of dress would be casual all day—easily adapted, for them, to plunging into the lake to swim, seemingly on instinct, or lying on the sundeck tanning. I soon wore trunks under my jeans and at times just trunks. Most days I would not bother to wear a shirt.

Earlier, I had heard the sound of exuberant laughter coming from the lake. That would be Sonya and Stanty, swimming, of course, or rowing, or both—I had seen them jump off the rowboat and swim away, then return to the boat later, perhaps racing.

Paul led me down the balustered stairway at the end of the main room. Not a basement, it was a full lower level of the house, a lower storey. We went into the library, a large room.

There were many shelves filled with books, some lying flat, space apparently exhausted. We walked along the aisles. The vast collection of books was not arranged in any discernible order; there were classics mixed with modern novels, some recently published—including one I had just read, William Styron's *Lie Down in Darkness*. I admired the book and was impressed by the fact that even its title conveyed its ominous tone. Faulkner, Thomas Wolfe, Conrad, Virginia Woolf. There were works on philosophy along with books on art, children's books—only those seemed to have been placed together in a neat group. Stanty's books, it amused me to think. There were reference books; books on religion, magic, witchcraft, history; poetry collections; T. S. Eliot's *The Waste Land*; Hart Crane; Flannery O'Connor, a favorite of mine—I felt that I shared her uproarious angry laughter at horrors. And, in French, Robbe-Grillet's *Le Voyeur* and *La Jalousie*, and other books whose titles I missed in a blur because I was trying to take it all in with hurried glances.

"You're welcome to take any book you want," Paul told me. "I put some in your room that I thought might interest you."

The man knew me only through brief exchanges and what he had read by me. A further manifestation of his arrogance.

Still, I would probably find his choices enticing—and revealing of him.

There was an equally eclectic collection of records, many left lying on the floor in their covers. I paused to look at some: symphonies, old and modern; operas, many jazz records—I noticed several by Ahmad Jamal—experimental music; rock and roll; Elvis Presley; Maria Callas; Fats Domino; Duke Ellington; *Noye's Fludde*; many by Edith Piaf; *El Amor Brujo*; Mozart; Kurt Weill; a full collection of Billie Holiday. I moved on to another shelf—I was not following Paul as he roamed among the stacks himself, pulling out a book, glancing at it, setting it aside. I was fascinated by the range of his collection. More: Schopenhauer, Dante—and Beauvoir, Sartre, Henry Miller, García Lorca, Beckett's *Malone Dies* and *Molloy*, Norman Mailer, Nietzsche—several volumes, two translations of *Beyond Good and Evil*. Inviting solitary reading, two small tables and a long one were matched by upholstered chairs. Everything, like the statues now departed from the lawn, suggested a reckless lavishness without design.

On a table, one book had been left open, facedown as if recently consulted, to be returned to. I read the title. *The Origin of Evil* by V. K. Edelstein, a name I thought I recognized, a book associated with controversy, maybe scandal. I would return to it later when I was alone.

"Island! Island!" The distant call came from the lake.

"Shall I leave you to choose some books?—or would you like to join me and Sonya on the sundeck? They're through swimming."

He was responding to the familiar signal. "I'll just look around the library now, then join you on the sundeck." My tan must be fading, his was deepening. But I was curious about the book left open on the table. It might be the book he had quoted from when we arrived, something about "evil."

After he was gone, I walked over to the book. Left open to tantalize me? Paul had known we would be roaming the library. There was a check mark on the margin next to this passage: "Four reflections. What one became, what the other will become, two bolts of lightning, opposites, on opposing sides. Intersecting, a point of explosive synergy where"—

I sensed a presence and turned. How long had Stanty been standing silently at the entrance to the library? I closed the book, turned to one of the shelves, and placed it in an open slot between other books, as if I had merely pulled it out and was now returning it. Why should I feel uncomfortable, as if he had caught me spying, when Paul had made the library available to me? I faced Stanty.

"Good morning, John Rechy," he smiled. "I was looking for you to ask you to go swimming with all of us." (Yet he had waited until I reacted to him.) "But maybe you—"

—don't know how to swim. In my mind I added the words I was sure he was about to say, an accusation.

"—prefer to read," he finished.

6

After I had left the library, thanking Stanty for his invitation and wishing that I had not withheld the fact that I didn't swim—a fact I knew would become obvious, if it was not already, and whose withholding, when revealed, would embarrass me—I went to my room to change into trunks.

I joined Paul and Sonya, drying each other after their swim, and, now, lying on pads under the sun.

"Good morning, my dear John."

I welcomed her ingratiating greeting. "Morning, Sonya."

"Hey, man."

"Hi, Paul . . . man."

Soon, the sundeck would become a place of congregation for us. For as long as we might abide the fierce heat (occasionally going to the small bar at the end of the deck sheltered there by a canopy and the shade of a large tree, its branches hovering over a demarcation and spilling into the sundeck while we drank water, chilled juice, and eventually Cuba libres, drinking and conversing), we would lie on lounging chairs, or—closer together—on pads, close enough to sense the heat of each other's body, as I am doing now, lying on a pad next to Sonya, not lying down yet, no, but sitting propped on my elbows to look at our bodies.

Next to me, Sonya is golden. Beside her rests the caftan she wears over her sunning suit when she leaves the sundeck, a veily, almost transparent covering that embraces her body. I can feel my tan darkening—soon surpassing Paul's, which is brown, the film of fine hairs on his oiled body turning blond. I detect the sweet scent of clean perspiration and mango-tinged tanning oil.

Paul sat up, to reach for a cigarette in the pack next to him. He has a unique way of smoking. He will light the cigarette, cupping it against a breeze even when there is none. He will inhale a few times, flip any ashes away, and quickly stub the cigarette on his palm, an action so quick and expert that he is never burned.

I looked away from him and lay back. I didn't want him to see me glancing at his body, in competition, not desire, no, only because my eyes, while comparing bodies, had noticed what seemed to indicate the prominence of his endowment. In my adult life, I have concentrated on my whole body as the object of attraction, but I am also secure with my endowment, and always competitive. Still, it annoyed me that Paul seemed to emphasize the bulge between his legs—but then, it was possible that his sunbathing next to Sonya, with the top of her bathing suit removed, accounted for a slight arousal, and therefore a misleading impression.

"I swam there today, all the way!" Stanty shouted as he appeared before us—and I began to think of his entrances as "appearances." He was dripping wet from swimming as he waited to make sure everyone noticed his presence.

When Sonya saw Stanty, she adjusted the upper part of her suit, covering her breasts, an endearing gesture of discretion.

"My darling, perhaps you rowed there?" Sonya said.

"Maybe. But I could have swum."

"Of course you could," said Paul.

"Of course," echoed Sonya.

It annoyed me that Stanty had interrupted sensual moments with his breathless declamation.

In an unsurprised tone that indicated a familiar reaction toward Stanty's claims, Paul said, "You went all the way to the island?"

"Yeah, and—" Stanty squatted next to us.

The neighboring island was apparently the basis for an evolving story by him, told and enhanced, to assert his bravery, as if he were the star in his fantasy play. "And—?" I was curious to hear his embellishment.

"I think there's someone still there," he said gravely.

"Who do you think it might be?" Paul coaxed out his story.

Stanty shook his head, as if considering the question seriously. "I think—you know." He pondered. "I don't know—I think there's something dangerous about that island."

"Stanty—" Sonya cautioned, in her kind tone.

Paul said easily: "Maybe you'd better stay away from there."

Stanty shrugged, ready to close his story on that hint of danger. I was sure that both Paul and Sonya pretended to believe his stories; he himself might not expect to be believed.

He sprang up, moved over to where I lay, and squatted next to me. In an urgent but lowered voice, a whisper that excluded the others, he said: "John Rechy, will you come with me? We'll row there and check that place out."

"Sure," I said, to placate him, "but not now."

"Okay, then, but soon," he said and walked away.

Had he wanted to tell me something private?—he had sought me out in the library earlier. I dismissed the thought and gave no credence to his fantasies.

7

Very soon I got to know much about Paul's life as he told it to me in long, surprising intervals I came to think of as "installments," not unlike chapters. His candor surprised me—it was exhibitionistic. He withheld nothing that was deeply personal in his "confessions"—no, not confessions, since he regretted nothing in the life he conveyed. His narratives might occur, start, or be continued on the deck facing the water, where we were now, after dinner, waiting for evening, drinking chilled wine, whose coolness did nothing to affect the heavy heat.

I noticed signals he gave to Sonya when he wanted to speak to me alone. He would begin talking slowly, then even more slowly, indicating he was rationing his words. She would smile, excuse herself, and leave, as she did now; and then he continued the saga of his life.

He called himself an "entrepreneur"—he pronounced that word with an ironic inflection that made me wonder whether he had assigned the word his own meaning. "And an art collector," he added, and paused as if waiting for me to ask for embellishment. I did not.

"The painting in your bedroom—you recognize it?" he asked.

"Of course." I withheld the name of the artist, resenting what seemed to be a test. "And the statues," I added.

"Beautiful, aren't they, man?"

"Very—and also ugly in a dark, twisted way, as if the soul has been squeezed out."

"Oh?"

Then he continued: His first wife—Elizabeth—was the daughter of the famous head of a prestigious law firm. The father's name came first on its letterhead; his wealth and notable ancestors allowed him entry into the highest social circles in the East—and anywhere else he might want to appear. His wife, Elizabeth's mother, was an independent woman long before that was widely accepted. She was a proud woman who disappeared periodically—informing her husband that she was in Europe and would return "soon," a fact that did not disturb the famous man, who was used to what others called her "eccentricities"—and what he referred to as part of her "ineffable charm" that included her refusal to adhere to any boundaries of what, in her elitist but markedly liberal background, was thought proper.

At the time when Paul met Elizabeth at a preferred university (where he had a full scholarship, information that he withheld from others, choosing to be identified as one of the select, attractive, and rich young men in the institution), "I gained a reputation as 'a young man of high potential and aspirations'"— he mocked the last words, pronouncing them as if they were the title of the story he was now telling me—or possibly a chapter in it: "A Young Man of High Potential and Aspirations." That contrived reputation and determination allowed him into the stratum of Elizabeth's parents. As a result, her autocratic father allowed his precious daughter to be courted by him. "He was," Paul said with malicious delight, "a rich, brilliant son of a bitch. He called my relationship with his daughter 'a reasonable match,' and he would add, 'An interim match,' not knowing how prophetic his attempted humor was. Later he called the match 'an abominable mistake based on that vulgar man's lies.' That was me, man," Paul added, laughing.

"I assumed that, man," I said, pleasing him, I knew, because I now easily used his word of street knowledgeability. "An Abominable Mistake"—that might be another title in the progression of his life.

He married Elizabeth. "She didn't care when she discovered that I was poor—it excited her to know that I had duped her father; she was rich, and that meant we were both rich," he said proudly.

After a period of "violent sex," they sank into "violent boredom." "It was only then that I got to know the insane woman I had married."

"Insane? Really insane?"

"You tell me, man. Listen." She was, he said, made crazy by those two powerful figures who insisted that she must have therapy in order to cope with them "intelligently." At their insistence, she began to consult a series of "progressive psychiatrists" beginning when she was nine years old. At her private school, she shocked other students and instructors by announcing that, soon, she would be dealing with her "disturbed alter ego," having acquired, she said, "peace for my own ego."

I laughed and he joined me, moving on to more.

"Elizabeth changed therapists with such regularity that often she forgot which idiot she would be talking to. Once," he went on joyfully, "she ran into her mother in the waiting room of that day's quack." Elizabeth discovered that distressing fact too late when the mother took the opportunity to tell her that—"because of the marvelous coincidence"—she had, just moments earlier, been discussing whether she and her eminent husband might be justified in "intercepting the marriage of her daughter to a monstrous fraud."

"That was you?" I interjected.

"Who else?" Paul said. "And if so," he went on, returning to the pending sentence, "might they be justified in proceeding to put into motion against him whatever extremity might be required, as long as—get this, man, the bitch actually said this and Elizabeth told me happily—as long as whatever they did was discreet and legal."

"I guess you were relieved to know she was excluding murder," I said.

"No, no, man. The stupid bitch didn't think murdering me could be illegal. She was as crazy as Elizabeth and their mutual quack, to whom she explained that all she wanted for her daughter was that she be rid of the monster—"

"You, Paul."

"Yes, man, yes—and then they would use all their connections to find her a desirable husband."

"Not you."

"But wait." He stopped to light a cigarette in his unusual way (and, I suspected, to create anticipation for his narrative), stubbing it out on the palm of his hand, not wincing. "Elizabeth finally found her 'savior,' the one and only Dr. Spitzer, known for his 'new radical therapy,' which had to do—listen to this, man—with 'adjusting one's psyche to ensure the balance of the universe by reverse interplay.'"

He waited for me to join in his laughter, and I did. "But who doesn't know all that?" I added to his derision.

"Beauty!" he called out abruptly, apparently having ended this installment of his life, which I titled in my mind "A Desirable Husband."

As—returning to offer more wine—Sonya bent over to refill Paul's glass, he raised his hands up to her so that the glass fell and shattered on the floor; both ignored that. Paul—roughly—brought her face down to his and they kissed hungrily, not passionately, but hungrily, their tongues probing, yes, hungrily. This display made me uncomfortable, although in my life I had indulged in public sex with men, in parks, on streets, in movie house balconies, and at times, challenged, in bright daylight; but those displays, mine, did not have what I felt seeing this union between Paul and Sonya: a twitch of fear, yes, fear; that is what I had felt at the violent connection, which, not surprisingly, revealed, when they parted, blood on Sonya's lips—she had winced in annoyance but did not wipe off the blood, and there remained, too, a smear of it on Paul's lips.

When the carnal connection had ceased Sonya—ignoring the shards of the broken glass—bent to fill my glass and, for a moment, I thought she would kiss me with the same ferocity, especially because she lingered in that close position, and I could smell the scent of her body and of the wine, and a whiff of something else.

That I was disappointed when she didn't kiss me, that I had reacted with such anger at their astonishing connection—that bothered me because I couldn't, at least not now, determine why it was so. An extension of my rivalry with Paul, now growing and spreading in every direction? That was it.

Still angry, I got up, retrieved the pieces of broken glass, and deposited them in Paul's ashtray on a small table beside him. The gathered shards of glass, their dangerous cutting edges, allowed a good termination to this night.

I lay in bed welcoming a breeze that went away too quickly. To extend its time, I had opened the door slightly to allow an easier flow, and perhaps a belated—but not really expected or desired—good night from Paul. Or Sonya. I sat up in bed, reading the book I had taken earlier from the library, Gertrude Stein's *Three Lives*; I was reading "Melanctha," loving its jazzy prose rhythms.

I found concentrating difficult. The subtle sounds of the island were mesmerizing, as if they were emerging from the lake . . . murmurs.

I tried to avoid glancing at the painting on the wall; but as I dozed off, I was aware that I was staring at it. It seemed to want to pull me deep into its vortex.

8

Our lives intersected randomly on the island. I say "randomly" although there had emerged a jagged pattern: We—one or another or even all; that is, Paul, Sonya, myself—might meet at breakfast. If I didn't encounter any of them then, I'd go to the library, reading whatever attracted me. Usually in the morning, Sonya and Paul went swimming, together or singly, or with Stanty. Throughout the day, each might dive into the water. When he was with them, Stanty would break away, swimming alone, far, far, concocting his extravagant stories to narrate later.

In the evening after returning from the sundeck to our rooms to shower, we would have the prepared dinner, together, and then retreat to the deck and face the lake. At any of the familiar locations, whomever we met, wherever we met, might determine whom we would be likely to linger with, and where, although the place often shifted, at times in mid-conversation; we might wander along the lawn, then lie down on towels on the grass. . . . Increasingly, and intuitively, we learned where each would be and when, and then the connection would occur, still qualifying as random.

I guess I should say that these planned "random meetings" excluded Stanty, who would materialize out of shady places. I imagined him listening, watching, waiting to assault us with excited exaggerations. It bothered me that I had begun to consider whether those tales, contradictory and incongruous as they might be, might not, at least in part, have even a grain of truth; and this consideration of possibility, at times, was followed for the briefest moment by a totally unwarranted apprehension.

If we had needed a reason for the scantiness of our daily clothing, the gasps of heat would have provided it. But, more, I thought, it was the island itself that determined, gradually and at first unnoticed, an intrinsic sense of abandon, a silent command of exposure.

Sonya roamed about the island in her misty creations like a beautiful dark butterfly. The erotic seminudity we adopted had not disturbed me; it pleased me—I was proud of my body, and so were Paul and Sonya of theirs.

Stanty—

—always in trunks or cutoffs. It was as if he was preparing to compete with me, with his developing body, as if he thought he was already the man he would eventually become, a man like his father. He swam endlessly or went rowing far away along the lake until he disappears.

At times, he would descend into the lower floor to the library, where eventually I would expect to encounter him— always with a brief greeting from him, returned. Our meetings are not entirely coincidental, since he must know the library is where I spend part of my time.

This morning is muggy. Dark clouds continued to promise rain but instead they floated across the sky and massed against the horizon, pasted there.

Earlier I had heard Sonya's and Paul's laughter—and
Stanty's childish hooting. I would be alone in the house.

Shirtless, my trunks under my Levi's in case I decided to
go later to the sundeck, I descended downstairs to the library,
the coolest location on the island. I roamed about the rich
collection of Paul's books. There was a beautifully bound set of
Remembrance of Things Past next to a historical novel by Frank
Yerby, a writer whose identity was kept secret because he was
black and wrote pulsing romantic novels of the Old South.
Nietzsche's *Thus Spake Zarathustra*, along with a volume by
Sade, and, next to that, *Das Kapital* and *Crime and Punishment*.
I intended to choose a book, maybe one I had not finished,
and sit at the long table to read. I pulled out a favorite from
my teen years, John Dos Passos's *U.S.A.*, whose literary tricks
and unconventional punctuation I had enjoyed. Not for today.
There was Joyce's *Ulysses*—which, when young, I had doggedly
read, every word of it, hardly understanding it until I reached
Molly's unabashed "soliloquy," which elated me so much that
I started the book again.

On that moody gray, hot day in Paul's library, I had been
putting off my real reason for being there—to retrieve the
book *The Origin of Evil*, which I had inserted between two
other books that I marked in my mind.

The book was gone.

Paul had probably been reading it—after all, it was likely
that this book was the one he had quoted from on the shore.
He had returned for it and taken it to his room.

I continued along the shelves, looking for a book that
would take my mind off the annoying absence. I pulled out
Wilde's *The Picture of Dorian Gray* to reread. As a freshman
in college in El Paso, I had chosen to write a required book

report on it. When the prim instructor interrogated me pri-
vately about my approach, I told her I felt sympathetic to Gray.
She denied that choice but agreed to my second one: *Paradise
Lost*. She returned the finished paper without a comment,
without a grade. I had made the case (not an original case, I
learned later) that Milton was on the side of the rebellious
angels, and I added that God was a frustrated tyrant secretly
in love with Lucifer.

Stanty.

Here he was now, with a towel wrapped about his trunks
and still wet from swimming. He nodded to me in salutation,
as if conforming to the rules of silence in a public library. I
nodded back and moved to another aisle, only to encounter
him again after a few minutes of wandering.

He sat at the long table, reading one of two or three books
he had chosen. I was curious to see what he was reading; but
with his lone silent presence in this room, I felt uncomfortable,
oddly trapped.

As I moved past him, intending to leave, he looked up
from his earnest reading and asked me, "Have you read Rimbaud, John Rechy?"

Rimbaud! "Yes."

"*Une Saison en Enfer*," he said. "*L'aimez-vous?*"

"Yes, I admire him"—though really not that much. I was
more intrigued with the poet's short life and his affair with
Verlaine, which was viewed so differently by each. "Do you?" I
asked Stanty. I would not comment on his showy use of French.

"No, I don't," he said firmly, as if he had caught me at
something he disapproved of. "Guess who—whom—I prefer?"

I wanted to be sarcastic, to mention a children's book,
maybe *Winnie-the-Pooh*, but that was a favorite of mine. I

couldn't think of anything else. "Who—whom?" I imitated his pretension.

"Baudelaire—*Les Fleurs du Mal*—he's much ... *starker.*"

"Starker?"

"You know—*stark,*" he responded nervously to my deliberate frown. "Rimbaud is so much more ... is ... lighter." He was looking at me as if to challenge me to question him, surely aware he hadn't chosen the words he intended.

"Oh. Lighter. Rimbaud is lighter. Baudelaire is stark."

Annoyed by my response, he slid two books aside. He reached for another book near him on the table. "Is this the book you were looking for?"

He held it up. *The Origin of Evil.*

"No," I said, "it's not. I was looking for another book and picked that one by mistake because it was on the table." I moved away from him.

Here he was again, but leaving. "Guess what, John Rechy? Sonya said she's going to make hamburgers." He rushed out, dragging the moist towel after him. He did not have any book with him.

It was not on the table. I searched the shelves nearby. Nowhere. Had *he* left it open the other day? His markings?

I stopped looking for it. I refused to be puzzled by a kid's odd game.

9

"We went to Constantinople," Paul continued, "trying to spike our lives with changing scenery, but Elizabeth continued to talk—endlessly—about her precious neuroses and her frightening insights."

We were lying on the sundeck under the violent glare of a white sun. It was a few days after Paul had delivered what I thought of as the first installment of his life—more to come. In a metaphoric rendering of that installment, "The Evening of the Shattered Glass" might be its title. Sonya had just left the sundeck—"to plunge into the water, cool water," she said. I had looked up at her, standing before us. The oil on her body had turned her into a perfect sculpture of burnished gold. Catching me staring at her, she had leaned over and kissed me on the lips.

"Sonya, Sonya!"

It was Stanty calling out to her, waiting to go swimming with her, and she left.

(I had learned from her that Stanty's bedroom was on the same wing as Paul's and mine, at the end of the corridor that connected us all. "At times, though," she said when I encountered her alone in the dining room at breakfast, "when he feels afraid, he stays with me until he falls asleep and I wake him."

("Stanty? Afraid?")

("Shhhh," she cautioned me. "He must never know I said that. Of course he's never afraid. Not Stanty. Never."

(She had retracted too quickly, assertively.

("But isn't he a little old to—?"

("No," she said emphatically, "not yet, not yet; and he stays with me—lying on a couch," she emphasized—"and only until he's falling asleep."

("But when Paul—?"

("Paul waits and sometimes carries him to his bed," she said, and added, as if I might consider her quick rebuttal angered: "I am so happy that you're here.")

Alone with me on the sundeck now, Paul had closed his eyes as if organizing his delivery. Lying next to him, I avoided looking at his body, or, rather, letting him notice me looking at it, still in comparison, a growing sense of competition. I had arrived at this acceptable deduction: I had developed muscles that indicated—not obtrusively—that I worked out with weights, whereas his body suggested his constant swimming. We were, therefore, even in our chosen body types. Still, there continued to be this: the ambiguous size of his endowment, which under his trunks—when Sonya was not there for me to attribute this to her sensual presence near him—was assertive. In Los Angeles, some homosexual men stuffed their groins under their tight pants; but since that was meant to attract others, I wondered how the impression was sustained when—if—they ended up in bed together.

"Our relationship entered another phase, necessarily. If we were to stay together any longer—though I don't know why we thought that was necessary—we would have to take extreme measures; we began 'playing games.'" Paul's laughter at stirred memories invited me to laugh, too, although I did not anticipate anything humorous.

We had left the sundeck sometime back when Stanty and Sonya had interrupted Paul's documentation of his and Elizabeth's games. We were now on the deck, waiting for sundown. I knew that Stanty would eventually burst in. He had an uncanny way of melding into whatever shadows had gathered, then springing out, like a piece of a shadow.

He was here now, on the deck. Did he wait—if he had all along been present and unseen—to interrupt at a chosen point?

"Is this the blue hour?" he asked me. That surprised me— his question, rendered pleasantly—because I remembered his disbelief about the existence of light and dark together when the subject of ambiguous dusk had first come up. He had arrogated that unique hour as something that was his own and, therefore, his to announce, and implicitly share at will.

"Not yet," I said. "When you detect it, will you tell us?" I did resent his interruptions when Paul had reached a point in his narrative where, like now, it seemed to me that something essential would be revealed. That was not only as a result of the intrinsic fascination his life invited; it was that, in his narration, I had felt all along that I would find a clue as to how he viewed me, how he had viewed me on his first contact with my writing, and especially why he had invited me here.

"I will," Stanty said, and stared ahead at the horizon to await the melding of lights, shifting his gaze intermittently, I noticed, to stare at the other side of the lake, where nightly the vacated island disappeared into darkness, an impression of tangled shadows.

His presence ended this evening's revelations; Paul and Elizabeth were once again left in Constantinople, an interruption that I suspected was greeted by Paul as an opportunity to retain suspense about the "games."

But that narrative was not kept in abeyance for long; only until the next day when we, Paul and I, were walking along the island before evening, in the late afternoon. Scattered about were wrought-iron benches located under thick branches of trees; at times, like now, we sat on one of the benches before continuing our walk.

Paul had resumed his narrative as if no time had elapsed between accounts, as if he were following the chapters of a book, in sequence, to be gone back to later where they had been left off. It was even, at times, as if he was finishing a sentence earlier left pending:

"—games that would provide new diversions in our ragged marriage." The last words were delivered with derisive disgust.

"She joined in the games," I said to indicate that, despite the elapsed time, his long asseverations, and the often loopy delivery that assumed its own order, I was following him.

As shadows lengthened along the lawn, I prepared myself for what I would soon hear as we resumed our walk.

"I had left our hotel to meet a woman who had introduced herself to both of us in a café."

"In Constantinople?" I said.

"There, yes, man. Elizabeth and I had competed for her for what would be a sexual liaison. I won."

"Of course," I said, emphasizing sarcasm.

"I went with the woman—a whore on her day off. Elizabeth would have done the same if the woman had chosen

her. Before I left, Elizabeth and I kissed to double the sensual
anticipation of a new encounter, bearing on our lips the taste
of each other to be shared with the vagrant partner, and that,
too, later shared by both of us. When I returned to the hotel to
meet Elizabeth, I didn't see her for long moments, until, with
a shrill screech like that of a siren sustained, she rushed at me
out of somewhere with a knife. After moments of struggling
I disarmed her—and she laughed. 'A new game,' she said. 'But
there has to be more,' I said. 'There is,' she agreed. She held the
knife out. I grasped it from her and we grappled and fought
over it until she succeeded in allowing the knife to cut into
her arm—"

"*She* succeeded, man?"

"It was a scuffle, man; who the hell knows who did what?
She held her arm up, letting a streak of dark red blood trickle
on herself. She did that, man, she did that," he laughed.

But I couldn't laugh. "You allowed that?"

"Of course, man. Now we were *both* playing. I fucked
her on the floor, while she held up her breasts to my lips for
me to lick the drops of blood that had dripped on her white,
beautiful breasts like rubies on her silky flesh."

At times like this, Paul repels me—not Paul, his life. I want
to assault his seeming indifferent cruelty, if that is what it is—I
have yet to determine what it really is. I can't deny my growing
fascination with him—with his life, that is. Even as he recounts
intimate details, he remains a mystery waiting to reveal himself,
if at all. And I have no doubt that he will reveal himself at the
right moment; and as I learned more about him, I knew that
moment—the accretion of all he had revealed—would come,
perhaps in silent violence, silent because as he was about to
shift to convey another development, his voice might descend

into a murmur, a whisper that became like a shout, delivered in a flood of angry words:

"Afterward, the fucken cunt said that what we had actually been involved in was 'reverse interplay'—she said that, man, she said it—and that we had achieved 'a psychic balance, exchanging guilt into extinction.' The fucken bitch said that, man; and I'm sure you recognize that she was shoving into the game the lunatic blathering of that crank Spitzer."

From the beginning of his narratives, I had wondered how accurately he was repeating words spoken to him and how much he was infusing them with his own contemptuous emphasis, although, often, he carefully attributed borrowed information to a possible and reliable witness. Whatever means he used, he narrated it all with staunch conviction, and I believed it.

"This is an excellent wine, don't you agree?" he asked me as we sat on the deck watching the darkness crawl over the lake.

"Yes, I do," I answered. "You have impeccable taste, man." I underplayed my compliment by adding "man."

When shadows had begun to stretch over the lawn, and we knew there would be no surcease from the heat this evening, we had returned from our walk to dinner with Sonya and Stanty. Dinner over, Sonya, having inferred that Paul wanted to converse with me—indeed, was eager to resume the pending installment of "Dangerous Games"—had asked Stanty to "escort" her to her quarters.

"Eventually, we traveled separately to augment the distance between us. But we returned to each other. That's when we met Corina in a club notorious for such meetings. In Constantinople." He smiled wryly, an indication that there was more to his emphasis than just the ancient name of a modern city of Istanbul.

"In Constantinople?" I goaded him to break his silence.

"Yes. Elizabeth's mother insisted on that name, Constanti- nople, where she went often. 'A city of surpassing grandeur and endurance against barbarity,' she insisted"—and he mimicked what was meant to be her exalted tone— "and she passed that insistence to Elizabeth; and so, man, it pleased the hell out of me when I discovered the notorious bar for the very wealthy to find any desired partner or partners in that very city. And that is where we met Corina."

"Of course." That was all I could think to contribute to his clear sense of delight at his discovery of such a place in the fabled city.

"Corina," he said. He paused as if to grant her a full entry into his narrative. "Corina, a beautiful woman who found money 'trashy' and was only too eager to squander it contemptuously."

"On you?" I said.

As if my question needed no answer, he turned over on the sundeck—where we had met the next morning, earlier than usual—his broad back as dark, I had to admit, as my chest. I remained facing up, feeling the sun licking my body, and, I supposed, his.

I had been anticipating an account of Stanty's birth or conception before Paul moved his narrative away from the place that had provided his son's hated name; and I waited, too, for a reference to the woman who bore him. But I would not commit myself to questioning Paul because I was sure that when he chose the right time to move there—if he did—the revelation would uncover the reason for the strange ambigu- ity about Stanty's mother, and I did not want to delve into turbulent waters.

"Elizabeth saw her first, standing in a light she had chosen, as she always did," he had continued. " 'You first,' I told Elizabeth. She went to the woman. I saw the two from the distance. I was sure they would leave together. But Elizabeth came back and said, 'She wants you.' I had recognized the woman; she was notorious for her beauty and for her father's 'trashy' wealth. Have you noticed, man, that wealth augments beauty? And notoriety augments both."

"And you succeeded in your conquest of both?"

"You tell me."

"Yes, you succeeded. And you eventually married her, beauty and wealth."

"I succeeded," he said.

He was using his technique of smoking in order to keep his narrative in abeyance. I took the opportunity to thwart that technique. I had waited long enough. "Why have you been telling me all this?"

He rolled over, propping himself up on one elbow to look at me. I opened my eyes, removed my sunglasses, and faced him.

"So that you will tell me as much about your own life."

"And that's the only reason?"

"Why else do you suppose, man?"

I could smell his lotion-tinged perspiration. "Okay, then, I'll tell you about my life . . . man. I was born in El Paso, Texas." I adopted an easy rote tone. "My mother was Mexican; my father was Scottish; he—"

Paul lay back facing the sun, his perspiration joining mine on the mat. "Come on, man," he chided me. "You know fucken well that's not what I meant."

Of course I had known that was not what he meant. At the very beginning of our conversations, he had lunged into accounts of his tumultuous marriages. "Yeah, man," I said, "I do know what you meant. But why would a big-time hustler like yourself—"

He laughed, appreciating my designation of him.

"—want to hear about the streets I prowled at midnight, and later, sometimes till dawn? Why would you want to hear about sex in dark alleys, hurried encounters in squashed rented rooms?—even mansions that reeked of paid sex and alleys, and at times it was only sex, just sex, only sex."

"You've convinced me that I want to know," he said. "Tell me about all that, everything. Your turn, man." He seemed excited; his words were urgent, pitched low, a demanding, intimate whisper. "What was it all about for you?"

"Hustling?"

"Yes! Being paid for sex with men."

"It was never about the money; at times no money was involved, just sex."

"Then what?"

"It was always about—" I had never asked that question of myself. "It was always about—" No word came, no answer.

"Power." He shoved the word at me; more words: "Power, of course, man, sexual power. You wanted power over willing victims."

10

Power over willing victims. I had winced at his words, which continued to echo, unwelcome. But why? They were *his* words, not mine; *his* deduction, not mine. Not mine? Had I trafficked on that dark street? Paul's words—uttered in admiration—kept resonating in judgement.

"—the blue hour."

"What?" I was startled by Sonya's words. She had walked onto the sundeck when Paul and I had been ready to leave— the heat had become unrelenting. I had been so immersed in the reverberations Paul's remark had set off in my mind that I had heard only a few words of her announcement. Standing before us waiting for us to respond, she looked like an apparition, rivulets of water like sequins on her darkened flesh.

"You said—didn't you, beauty?—that Stanty has a surprise he wants to reveal during the blue hour."

"Yes, after dinner," Sonya said.

Paul laughed, surely at Stanty's dramatic presentation of his supposed surprise.

I was sure the "surprise" would be another exaggeration of his ventures into the neighboring island, graver intimations of looming dangers.

At the announced time, as we sat on the deck trying to ward off the sullen heat with chilled wine, we learned Stanty's surprise as the bluish cast of evening brought down the night.

"If the blue hour is when everything is the way it really is"—standing assertively before us—"then we should take advantage of it, shouldn't we?"

"How do you suggest?" Paul indulged him.

"By telling secrets."

"How do you play that?" Sonya said.

"Very simple." Stanty remained facing us, taking command.

I resented his demand that we attend to what would surely be a disappointing revelation I resented Paul's—and Sonya's—permision of his brazen charade; and yet, annoyed, I was curious to hear what he would say.

"Everyone has to tell a secret," Stanty instructed.

"Oh, Stanty—" Sonya dismissed. but in a kind tone.

"Please!" he said. "Father?"

I hoped Paul would reject the suggestion. He didn't, watching his son intently as I now expected he would when Stanty "performed," studying him.

"First you'll have to tell us why you chose that game," Paul said.

I needed to ambush their alliance before this proceeded. "I think Stanty is eager to reveal his own surprise and so he's made this game up. Why not get to that first?"

He answered Paul: "Because it's getting to be the blue hour, and that's the time when everything is revealed." He turned to me: "Isn't that so, John Rechy? Remember what you said?" He was adjusting his game. "You first, Father. Please, Father, please."

"This is my secret," Paul said, "I love—"

The word jarred me, so incongruous for him not only now but at all. When he had spoken those words, he had fixed his stare on Sonya, a locked stare, with a smile.

She answered back, an unwincing stare, a challenge—I sensed it—between them.

"I love . . . Stanty, very much," Paul finished, and broke the stare. "And—"

"That's no secret, that you love me, you're my father, you have to love me, and I love you, so much, Father. You have to go again."

Paul said, "You can't change rules in the middle of the game."

"And—?" Sonya goaded Paul to finish his declaration.

He shrugged, silent.

She had risked Paul's dismissal, prodding him to add her name to his declaration.

"You have to go again, Father," Stanty insisted. "You have to reveal a *real* secret." He assumed a rigid pose, adding to his insistence: "Father!" The pose broke. "Father?" he pleaded, staring at Paul, Paul looking back at him, silent; and silent intense moments passed.

There was a clear purpose in Stanty's game, I was sure. There was something specific he was calling for from Paul while disguising it by bringing the others into his game. Sitting next to me, Sonya sensed that; her hand on mine was tense.

"Father!" Stanty demanded. "Who is—?"

"It's John Rechy's turn," Paul interrupted sharply.

The first time he had used that tone with Stanty. Whatever had occurred between them remained like an echo without discernible origin.

Stanty regained control. "Okay, then. John Rechy, you're next," he proceeded.

Did he want to prod me into the embarrassing announcement that I had withheld, that I didn't know how to swim? He had implied asking that before. Fuck the little bastard. I would make this my opportunity to assuage Sonya, get back at Paul for his rejection of her.

I said. "This is my secret: I love Sonya."

"Your magic powers reign, beauty," Paul dismissed my comment.

"Love? Or in love?" Stanty pushed on.

"I meant love," I said. I should have said "in love." That's what Sonya would have preferred, to counter Paul's omission of her.

"Sonya," Stanty called on her.

"My secret? My secret is that I have no secrets."

"That doesn't make sense," Stanty said softly.

"It does," I said, to ward him off. Her hand on mine was gentle.

She said: "Now you, Stanty, what's your secret?"

"He has so many he won't remember just one," I said.

Whatever "secret" he had, he didn't seem ready. The game had run away from his intentions.

"Game's over!" he announced, and he jumped upon the wooden border that enclosed the deck; and, with his arms up, hands pointing in the stance of a champion swimmer, he lunged into the dark water.

"Stanty!" Paul shouted.

"Stanty!" Sonya echoed.

Both jumped up to look over the railing, aware of the boats bound beneath us, the possibility that he would fall on one of them, hard.

We heard a splash, the gurgle of water, and then words over the splattering as he swam outward:

"Island! Island!"

11

Yesterday or the day before—time is fluid on the island—I woke up late to find a note under my door from Sonya. They—I assumed she and Stanty and Paul—were driving into the village early in the morning to check on some electric fans that Paul had ordered, fans necessitated for the first time on the island because of the relentless heat.

I decided this was an opportunity to teach myself how to row, surely not difficult. I didn't want to expose myself to the awkwardness of being taught. I pushed one of the boats a short distance into the lake. As I began to board, the boat seemed to pull me in, and then it began to rock and push forward as if to take control and of its own volition direct me to the vacated island, which, each time my eyes involuntarily sought it out—like now—appeared more dour than before. I postponed my attempt at rowing for another time.

I am looking for Paul to continue the suspended account of his and Elizabeth's competing for Corina. During our latest conversation when he had expressed his desire to know about the aspect of my life that intrigued him, I had contributed nothing after he had interrupted my words with his disturbing evaluation.

I am becoming aware that events that assume importance when they occur are assigned a finality on this island. That was so with Stanty's dangerous jump into the dark water. Not a word about it had followed.

I ran into Sonya outside. "They've gone into the village to see whether the fans have finally arrived," she told me when she assumed I was looking for Paul. She held my hand playfully and moved me along with her. "Let's go rowing, we'll be alone on the boat, you and I, on the beautiful serene lake."

It delighted me to believe that she had stayed behind in order to be with me; but, concerned about the possibility that she would sense my awkwardness at rowing and attempt to teach me, I said, "Let's take a walk instead."

It was near noon, and Sonya and I wandered among the trees and the flowers miraculously surviving the heat. Sonya's thin caftan drifted behind her like colored wings as she walked and then it quickly wrapped intimately about her body. As she became darker from the steady sun, she was even more beautiful. (I was fascinated by her lips, which even without makeup were deep red, sensual, as glossy as fresh blood.)

Too hot even for a walk, we lay under a cluster of shading trees on towels she had carried from the sundeck. The slight awkwardness that followed reminded me that this was the first time we had been alone without the expectation that either Paul or Stanty would appear.

Sonya spoke about her family in France, where she was born; how she was "discovered" by the famous designer Julian

Arvayon and became a fashion model, a fact that did not surprise me.

"And then I met Paul."

"And——?"

"And then I met Paul," she repeated, as if that was all she
needed to define her recent life.

Her abrupt reticence annoyed me, as if she was with-
drawing her trust; I wanted to consider her an "ally" although
I wouldn't be able to identify opposing parties. Too, she had
introduced an essential subject, how she had met Paul.

Interpreting my silence as annoyance with her seeming
evasion—a long silence that seemed laden with stagnant heat—
she said: "Paul was divorced from both women, or about to
be, I forget. I was modeling for Arvayon, an imperious fashion
designer—and an infamous unpaid pimp. He introduced men
and women—and, yes, he was a friend of Paul's. Paul knew
everyone. Julian was having an important show. Paul asked to
attend. I did not know I was for sale. He was there to choose
from the line of women on the runway. He asked Julian to
introduce him to me. Julian did. That was it. We traveled, we
made love—oh, no, we had sex, a lot of sex. We traveled more,
we had sex, more sex, and here I am."

She had felt bought, but apparently she had lasted long
enough to feel confident of enduring. "Now, you must tell me
how he summoned you."

Summoned? Had he referred to his inviting me here as
"summoning" me? "He read something I had written, and he
admired it. He invited me here." What more did she know than
I did about how he saw me? I moved away from the subject
she had deliberately or inadvertently introduced. I told her
about my background in Texas.

"How erotic Texas must be!" she said.

I was sure she had meant "exotic," but I followed through: "Maybe, if you find cactus and deserts erotic, sensual."

"I do," she said, miming a tremble of excitement. "I find it very . . . sexual, especially since that's where you're from. What do you think of Paul?"

Like that, she ended the prattle, not allowing me to respond to her flirtatious remark. "I think he's a fascinating man. He's certainly intelligent, I enjoy our conversations."

"I love him very much," she said.

Considering the way Paul had spoken about his wives, I wondered how he would describe his feelings for her. I was beginning to feel protective of her.

Sonya closed her eyes as if that enabled her to continue: "He's a fantastic lover." She turned her head away from me, briefly, an unexpected reaction of shyness. "But," she continued as if she had rehearsed the words but had kept them to herself until now, "not once has he spoken a word of true affection—and never the word . . . love. I spoke it myself finally, and he pushed me away from him, furious."

Although I winced at the evoked rejection, I could understand an aversion to the word "love." It was difficult for me to reconcile sex and love. They existed separately; one interfered with the other. Love neutered desire. I had fled Los Angeles in part because of such contradictions.

"I'm exaggerating my feelings." She laughed. "He accuses me of that, when I'm able to mention feelings at all. I'm telling you this because I need to put it into words, speak it, and because I feel a closeness with you."

She, too, needed an ally in whatever she might be considering. The enraged kisses with Paul that I had witnessed—they recurred as if on irresistible impulse, a violent impulse; he would clasp her to him to kiss her, a devouring kiss asserting ownership.

"I'm glad you're telling me this." I wanted to reassure her that I, too, felt close to her, but I couldn't say that, not now—not yet—although she seemed to be waiting for me to speak.

"Is it true that you have been a prostitute?" she asked me.

I was startled by the question. I wasn't ready to discuss that part of my life with her—not now, perhaps another time. Apparently Paul had mentioned this to her, and perhaps given her my stories to read.

"I never considered myself that," I said. "It's somewhat different, between men—"

"Only men were involved?"

Surely Paul would have told her that. "Yes—only men, and I never felt like a prostitute. We call it hustling."

"But you were paid—by men—for sex?" she pursued.

"Yes. But not always. Sonya—" I wanted to end this conversation.

"But I find that so exciting!" she said.

"I don't want . . ." It wasn't shame or embarrassment that made me reticent—I saw no reason to feel either; I just didn't want to move away from information about Paul and their relationship.

"I suppose you could say that Paul is a . . . hustler? His rich wife Corina paid him grandly when they divorced, wouldn't you say?"

"That's called alimony," I laughed.

"I believe Paul is the first man who ever collected alimony. The statues, the paintings. And this island—it was her father's retreat, then hers." She laughed mirthlessly. "Corina! The notorious heiress to one of the great American fortunes. Perhaps it was payment that she gave him."

"Island! Island!" It was Paul's voice, distant, calling from the shoreline.

Then Stanty answered with the same two words, startling me because Sonya had indicated he had gone with Paul. Then we were not alone.

"Paul's signal that he's back," Sonya said, noticing the direction of my attention. "That call binds them," she went on; "a place entirely theirs, a world they both rule."

"Paul seems to study Stanty, almost in fascination with his own son," I said, taking the opportunity to know whether she noticed that, and perhaps why; or was that only in my imagination? "He supports Stanty's lies, like about the other island."

"Stanty is a creative boy, and very smart. Most of his stories are exaggerations; we accept them as such, and I believe he knows that. Telling adventurous tales, that's not exceptional for a boy his age, is it?—to fantasize a mystery?"

"No, it isn't." Truly, the murky atmosphere that surrounded the unoccupied island did invite heightened conjecture. Though his versions of his treks to the neighboring island might change, the fact of his having gone there remained.

"Stanty's closeness to his father comes from the fact that his mother—"

"Elizabeth—" I said.

"Or Corina, I'm not sure, and Stanty doesn't—"

She stopped abruptly. She seemed to have surprised herself with the blocked words. I waited for her to go on. "Sonya?"

"They may both come," she said.

"Do you resent that?" What did she withhold about Stanty's mother? Something that echoed Stanty's halting demand of Paul on the night of "secrets"?

"Paul asked me whether it upset me that they might come, and I said it did not, because I know he fears being possessed in any way, owned." She held her breath, preparing, I knew, to speak a painful truth: "I know that if I opposed his wishes, he might even— His anger, it's overwhelming when he's opposed."

He might even leave me? Whatever she had intended to say, it was a suspicion so painful that she couldn't enunciate it; and I didn't want to hear it.

I'd had relationships with women that I thought of as "love affairs," love affairs without sex. They were much closer than friendships—stronger and more lasting—and more intimate than the few brief relationships I had allowed with men, gay or not. With Sonya there might be—I thought at some moments—even more.

She moved close to me as if sensing a need for protection. I was keenly aware of her, the bronzed body glowing in the shade. I wanted to draw even closer to her. But I did not.

What she had just revealed, the anger in her love of Paul, and something withheld about Stanty's mother, and the possibility that both of Paul's ex-wives might come to the island—all added to the perception of secrets waiting for revelation; and those pressurized revelations might come—the startling image invaded my mind—in a burst of darkness and heat; and at the same time as the violent vision I had conjured came, I knew I was waiting for something—as vague as that, "something"—that might explain why I had been "summoned" here.

"You must, you know"—the pained rage had disappeared from Sonya's face—"learn to swim, John. It's essential when you're living on an island. Surrounded by water."

12

Night had brought no relief from the heat. The night was sweating. A mass of lightning-punctured clouds gathered on the horizon, promising rain but bringing only moisture and the rumbling of thunder.

It seemed to me—now acutely but only at times—that the island existed only for us, the three of us: no, the four of us. We would separate at times, only to come together again, as if powerfully drawn back. Stanty often disappeared into dark clusters of trees, under which, I imagined, he slept, stroked by shadows, imagining—what?

The gray couple drifted about as if they did not exist.

Paul and I sat on the back deck, drinking the chilled wine he had just opened. He had remarked cursorily that he had not seen me all day—he had just returned from the village, where, still, no electric fans were available. I told him Sonya and I had taken a walk on the island. I did not perceive that he was suspicious or angry at our being together; he seemed to welcome it. "Good," he said. Of course, there was nothing to suspect.

He had returned to his account of the turbulence between him and Elizabeth, leaving Corina on display under a golden spill of light in the notorious club in Constantinople. It continued to be startling, the way he so easily delivered—and slipped into—the intimate aspects of his relationships. "Elizabeth was like a dog in heat," he said. "Before we married, she was prim—pretending, of course; she claimed she was a virgin, she kept her legs crossed tightly even when we were at dinner. But she changed into a dog in heat. She devoured me—"

"And you—?"

"Loved it, of course, and devoured her back." He was smoking—indulging in more puffs than usual; the smoke floated out gray toward the water.

"Dear Paul," Sonya said, overhearing, "it's you who fuck like a fantastic dog in heat, my beautiful beloved"—and she laughed.

Paul looked up at her, not laughing. In trunks as usual, he stretched his long, tanned legs out as if to display them.

I turned away from what seemed to me to be an exhibition. Shirtless. I tensed my body.

That was the first time I had heard Sonya even jokingly rebut Paul, although she had tempered her words—"a fantastic dog." Perhaps, after our long talk on the grass when she had revealed her apprehensions, she had become emboldened to challenge him. Or to warn him with hyperbole—"beautiful beloved"—of her own capacity for anger. It pleased me to believe that I might have had something to do with her reaction.

She leaned back, her head tilted up, and—more like a wolf than a dog—"Is this how she sounded, Paul?" She brayed: "Awoooooo, awoooooo."

"Stop that, bitch," Paul said, "Stanty will think you're calling him."

I laughed at that; so did Sonya. Of course, Stanty might suspect the wolf's call was a call to him. Paul had not laughed.

"What's funny, beauty?" He turned to Sonya.

I answered for her and myself: "Stanty," I said; "you calling him a wolf. I'd be careful if I were you, man—with his imagination he might start claiming to be one." No laughter, best to leave it there. Still laughing, Sonya had gone back into the house.

And there he was, Stanty appearing on the deck asking whether he had missed the blue hour. (I chose not to ask whether the "wolf call" had summoned him.) "You did ask me, you know," he addressed me. "You told me. Remember, John Rechy?" he said. "You told me to tell you when it was the blue hour."

A few nights ago I had told him that. "Well, you already did."

He leaned over the railing—a bluish darkness was creeping over the lake. He was determined to assert his assumed role as announcer. He whipped around. "You lied, John Rechy."

Paul did not move, did not look up, remained impassive in his chair.

"How?" I said.

"When you said that the blue hour revealed the truth about lies. It hasn't, it doesn't. It's just a damn silly story you told. Nothing different has happened." Then, in the same strange pleading voice I had heard before, he said to Paul, softly: "Has it, Father?—just a silly story?" He waited, expectant.

I, too, waited for Paul to answer the urgent question—and to rebut the accusation that I had lied.

But all he said was, "Oh?"

Stanty stood in front of me, demanding an answer.

"I guess you have to wait for that to happen," I said, to mollify him; "not right away, not every time, and you did come up with a game—I believe you called it 'playing secrets.' "

"I saw you!" he said to me.

Paul sat up.

"Saw me what?" I asked Stanty.

"With Sonya! On the grass." He turned to Paul. "They didn't know I could see them. Father, he kept pushing himself against her, on the grass, he wouldn't let her go, she kept pushing him away—and he kept on, and then he even—"

"You're a fucken liar!" I stood in front of him. I looked at Paul to gauge his reaction.

He was smiling, amused! "And how did that make you feel, Stanty?"

Even Stanty seemed bewildered by the question. "It—I—"

"You know that isn't true, Stanty." It was Sonya—overhearing—and she had spoken to him gently, with nothing harsh in her tone. She walked over to him and touched him briefly on his arm.

"I wonder how it would feel, Stanty," Paul said, reclining back in his chair, "to apologize to . . . John Rechy?"

Stanty smiled, a broad smile. "Just joshing with you, John Rechy. You knew that all along, didn't you? You did, didn't you, Father, know I was joshing, didn't you, Father?"

"I did, yes, I did."

"And I bet Sonya knew that, too."

"Of course I did," she said, smiling back.

"John Rechy, you knew that, too, didn't you? Didn't you?" he insisted.

I sat back in my chair, looking at him. He was smiling at me as if indeed he had been only "joshing," and once again he was the playful kid. I did not answer him. I wondered how far his tales might take him, and at what point they might be believed.

13

Elizabeth and he were bound by "passionate hatred," Paul explained the next day, still abandoning Corina under a stunning light in a notorious bar. We are sitting at the big dining table, where we have just had breakfast, feasting now on purple grapes. "If we separated, we wouldn't be able to torture each other so easily. We were not yet through."

"Still in Constantinople?"

"Yes, yes," he said, and went on with what Elizabeth had told him: "'If you killed me,' she proposed, 'I would die ecstatic.' I did not ask her why; she was eager to tell me: 'Because I would know that you would be sent to prison, probably for life, and forced to wear a drab uniform, probably striped, and made to live in a cramped disgusting cell,' she said, licking her lips, as if she could taste the pleasure that would bring her. 'Or'—she went on, inspired—'perhaps, you would be executed in the electric chair.' She made a hissing sound in my ear, imagining the electric current that would sizzle through my body. I said to her, 'I'll be sure never to kill you. But, then, Elizabeth'—this had occurred to me and I was excited to say it, to trap her—'how would you balance the universe if I were to kill you? It would remain askew, chaotic. I'm sure that Dr. Spitzer would agree and be outraged. The only way to retain the balance of the universe—which is your noble goal and Dr. Spitzer's, isn't it?—would be for you, then, to kill me and *you* would go to prison, forced to wear an ugly uniform, probably striped, and live in a cramped, disgusting cell. But that wouldn't be possible, would it?—since I had already killed you.' I had upset her stupid game; I knew she would be discussing it at length with her quack doctor, the author, believe me, of his second self-published book, *A Radical Theory 2: Permanently Retaining the Psychic Balance.*" He laughed raucously.

I laughed, too, at the absurd situation he had delineated with contempt—and, too, at the trap Elizabeth had set for herself in the proposed entertainment.

"Elizabeth and I celebrated our separation." Paul picked up his account when we were sipping wine on the deck after dinner. " 'No, no,' she said, 'not with champagne. With cheap whiskey, that's what our marriage calls for—the cheapest whiskey'—and that's what we drank."

Later than usual, Sonya and Stanty had gone swimming, attempting to cool off from the hovering heat. I envied their exuberant shouts and laughter, which I listened for.

"But, man," I ventured, "out of all that, what finally made you leave Elizabeth?"

He looked at me as if befuddled by an obvious question. "Because," he said emphatically, "she *was*." His frown eased. "Because she *existed*, that's all."

He was so fucking sure of himself and everything he said. (He had located himself so that his angular profile was etched against the dim moonlight, which struggled out of sudden dark clouds.) "But you fell in love again, with Corina?" I thought that would annoy him, the assumption that he could "fall in love," as much as he must detest that phrase.

Instead: "Yes, deeply," he said, perhaps because he had figured out my intention. "I fell in love with her when I first saw her."

"In the notorious club where she was standing under a display of light," I furnished the rest.

He said, thoughtfully: "I did fall in love with Corina. No." He backed off. "I fell in love with her beauty. I loved her fucken beauty—"

"—and her wealth," I said.

"Of course, man," he said, unperturbed.

Would he soon move on to deride Sonya? I had seen hints of her rebellion. I was becoming apprehensive when he insulted his wives so brashly, because I didn't want to hear anything like that about Sonya.

Yet despite my recurrent trepidation of where his anger might lead him in his ranting—we were drinking the same white wine we had at dinner—I was feeling, this hot night, the camaraderie that occurs between people drinking together, feeling that camaraderie, and quite as powerfully rejecting it.

I heard a vague stirring at the dark edge of the deck. It would be Stanty—back from his swimming with Sonya and eager to irritate us in some way. He would have been hiding, listening—as he had been when he saw me and Sonya lying on the grass. No, it was the sound of a boat on the lake. A startling breeze had swept onto the deck accompanied by the sound of water stirring, a coolness soon banished by an ambush of heat.

With my silence, I encouraged Paul to continue his saga, and he did, but still without any reference to Stanty's birth although his narrative was departing from Constantinople.

Corina, the beautiful young heiress, claimed to be superb at betting on new artists before they were "discovered widely," Paul said. "She told me she was 'collecting tomorrow's great art.' What she was actually collecting was today's fake art. She had a refined talent for buying bad but expensive forgeries. I guided her away from her reckless purchases; I advised her carefully because I knew that eventually I would claim all the art as mine."

"What a cunning son of a bitch you are."

He was pleased: "Yes, I lived by my wits—like you, man."

I added to my conjectures about his motive in inviting me: he was "collecting" artists—a "promising" young writer—and courting an allegiance to him.

"Throughout all your sexual encounters, man, did you ever steal?" he asked me.

"Yes," I answered truthfully.

"Then you, too, are a son of a bitch," he drew his equation.

I resented the connection he was trying to establish between us. There had been again an intimation of judgement— for him, a welcome cherished judgement, a celebration of his cunning. But his self-approving judgement had once again stirred another judgement, a powerful one, on myself. I would have to extricate myself from any overlapping of our lives, an overlap he seemed determined to assert.

"How did you feel after you stole?" he asked.

"Sometimes . . . guilty," I said. The word had come easily in answer to his question; but as it echoed—and it did echo in my mind—I knew I had lied. In all those fleeting encounters, I had felt a sense of triumph to be desired on my terms, nothing else.

"Guilty!" Paul rejected. "For stealing from willing victims?"

Willing victims—again. His claim jolted me anew. Later, I would explore my feelings about what he had deduced, what I had really felt about guilt and non-guilt, and why I felt either. Or neither.

"Your turn," he said.

Did he imagine he would go slumming through my memories of hustling turfs? His silence awaited a response. But I didn't want to explore what he was asking for. I said I preferred that he continue with his narrative.

"Your turn, man," he insisted. "The streets, the alleys, the sex ..."

It was my turn, yes—my turn to match his maneuver of extending interest by delivering installments left pending at a dramatic high, the inception of a crisis.

"I was arrested once for—" I halted. "You go on, man," I said.

14

Often, Paul plays music on the hidden stereo—the music is his choice and unpredictable, although he sometimes asks for requests. Music floats over the island through speakers onto the back deck after dinner and onto the sundeck, where he and I are reclining on mats, sweating, although we came out early attempting futilely to stave off the heat. Today's invisible music is from Weill's *The Threepenny Opera*, Lotte Lenya rasping out Brecht's lyrics. I know from their pursuing laughter that Stanty and Sonya are rowing and now and then diving into the water to swim.

The Threepenny Opera ends, and Paul says, "I enjoyed fucking Corina's millions."

"You really did that, man? Fucked her millions?" I taunted.

"Yes. Listen, man. I took all the bills she had with her—she carried hundreds—and I scattered them over her naked body; yeah, I even stuffed some between her legs. I straddled her and jerked off over her and her money. She rubbed my cum and her money all over herself and laughed, 'Filthy, filthy.'"

Regretting my question, I turned over on my stomach, to tan my back. A fine film of perspiration and oil glistened on my body and his.

"My cum all over her fucken money—her filthy money."

A bastard, a fucking bragging bastard. Yet—this baffled me, and disturbed me—I "liked" him. I couldn't think of another word as he continued recounting his excesses. I was fascinated by his heated recollections, even though at times they angered me—and at other times baffled me, like now when he said:

"Once, man, I tested her about how filthy her money was. We were in Italy. There were beggars on the street, tattered men and women, and dirty, ragged children. I dug into her purse and scattered money on the street. They all scrambled for the money, but—get this—the merchants in the shops rushed out, pushing the vagrants away, snatching the money from them, knocking down the children. Your clowning demonic angels at their best, man, fighting for filthy beads!"

Not beads. Money. I had recognized a similarity between his story and mine in "Mardi Gras"—the costumed revelers I had depicted scrounging for beads; and I had detected sudden anger in his voice as he recalled the ugly scene. Anger at whom? Not the beggars, surely. At Corina? The shop owners? Or at himself for flaunting money to prove his disgust with it all?

"And what did Corina do?" I said.

"What else, man? She laughed drunkenly. She was always drunk." As if to wipe away the street image he had evoked—and perhaps his startling anger—he shifted his position, facing me, and I shifted mine to face him, both leaning on our elbows.

"What were you arrested for?"

"Hustling. I was inexperienced. A vice cop offered me money and then busted me."

"You went to jail?"

"A friend bailed me out the same night, and I went home with him and hustled for the bail."

"Good, man, good," he approved.

He was disappointed, as I had suspected when I tantalized him about that event. He would have preferred a long prison term and a harrowing account of depravity. The reality of it was as grim, but I didn't want to remember it. The island seemed to negate concerns beyond its perimeter. No, I did not tell him about the raids on gay bars; cops invading private homes to arrest men having sex, the sexual act being illegal; entrapment, lying, aroused cops, years-long prison terms, suicides, violence. I had been the exception in the quagmire of depraved laws—which ironically allowed a powerful attorney "with high connections" hired by my friend to get me off with two years in prison, suspended; and probation for the suspended time, probation I ignored in defiance of the rotten laws.

"But—" I tried sarcastically to assuage Paul's heated anticipation—"that one night in jail, man, whew; I can't even talk about it." I left it there for his imagination.

Taking two puffs from a cigarette, waving away an intrusive wisp of smoke, he said: "As I read what you wrote, I didn't realize until later that you shifted from past to present tense in the same sentence. What effect were you after?"

Following the confounding story he had told about the scattered money—and it would haunt me and I would try to decipher its meaning for him—and following the embittering memory of my arrest, I welcomed the new conversation. "I wanted to dismiss the separation between past and present, and, yes, the future, to assert an even level of time; and this, too ... man"—I softened my too-passionate defense—"there's no demarcation between time in memory, is there? And aren't there memories that push into the present, so powerfully that they become a part of the present? That's what I'm trying for in some shifts, and—and—" I waited for him to respond, agreeing or dismissing.

"I get that, man," he said finally, with what I chose to believe was a touch of enthusiasm. "But"—I anticipated some rebuttal—"the infrequent capitalization?"

I shoved away a feeling that he had been about to grade me. I wouldn't let that intrude on our conversation; I was basking in it. "I was trying out visual effects on the page like, I believe, in some editions of *Winnie-the-Pooh*."

He laughed. "You mentioned that book before and you were serious?"

"Why should a writer limit his influences? I've been influenced by movies, good and bad: the abrupt shifts in location, dialogue like a voice-over along with shifting scenery—special effects in narrative, man. Look how Buñuel slides from realism to surrealism with only gradual clues of that shift; and I like to listen to music before I write, like Fats Domino and then Mozart, something like Eisenstein's montage, in music, juxtaposing opposites, tension, and—"

We're lying on towels on the grass of the expansive, expensive lawn under the shade of a tree allowing the impression of coolness. We left the sundeck when the heat became violent.

"—movie serials influenced me a lot, like pushing a character into a trap that seems impossible to escape and than letting him spring out, like Flash Gordon—and comic books, their exclamatory prose. *Batman*—I never cared for the boy Robin. I loved Saturday-morning movie serials, man, learning about suspense, adding details to deepen a mystery, not just withholding." I was rushing on, breathless, excited, as if to make up for the years when I had separated myself into another world, where I played someone else, only street-smart. "—and take the power of suggestion in Val Lewton's great B movies, and look at *Cat People*—an ominous shadow on the pool wall, growing darker, larger as it seems to approach the woman swimming, the water shimmers like shards of glass, which are always good for arousing tension, like in *Persona*, the broken glass and the actress walking past it, missing it—"

"—like Hitchcock letting the viewer in on danger the character doesn't perceive, no?"

I liked his apparent agreement, but I didn't like his arrogating my direction. "That's an easy deduction," I dismissed his remark, and aimed at him: "—and I picked up on the use of gestures as characterization, like the way you smoke, Paul, the way you—"

"Oh?"

That irritating "Oh." "—snuff out a cigarette as if you—"

"Yes?"

I'd leave it there, taunting him. "Mathematics, too, a big influence. In high school, I—"

"Mathematics?"

"—was fascinated by the shape of algebraic equations plotted on a graph, the intersection of lines makes an X, man, and that's the solution to the equation. It's like two narrative currents that intersect at a point of possible reconciliation—the mysterious X, and—"

"You're breathless, and you're not making sense."

"—then splitting apart." I had leaped over his insult. I caught up with it, angered: "Fuck if I'm breathless, fuck if I'm not making sense."

He laughed. I joined him. "Okay, man, I'm convinced," he said. "You're good, man."

What can I say to this man who has, correctly—almost correctly—understood my intentions and is responding in admiration? Yes, what can I say, except what I do say, which is:

"Thank you, Paul."

He fell back into the stream of his life:

"Corina was frigid."

15

"Fuck you, man. You bragged that you fucked and fucked—your words, man."

"The fucken bitch was a liar. She told me I was the only man who could 'tame her heat.' So she possessed me with desire, and, yes, we fucked and fucked, and she trembled and groaned. Then one time after hundreds—she fell back, exhausted, crying. She formed a fist and she struck her cunt with it, over and over. 'A piece of dead meat! Cold, frigid!' she screamed between sobs."

I felt pity for the woman I had never met. He, too, must have felt her sadness, her pain—I waited to hear him say how he had pacified her. I waited.

He lit a cigarette. He inhaled, exhaled, three puffs this time, studying the wisp of smoke that drifted into the shaded heat. "With the revelation of her lie, I knew that if I was to acquire her wealth when I divorced her, I would have to thaw—to crack—the locked, frozen cunt. Nothing else would guarantee my success."

The harsh vulgarity of his delivery about the woman he had married jarred me. It was as if his sexual relations required a different language, a degrading language of their own. That, and the indifference with which he described his selfish motives, at times repelled me. And yet my desire to hear more—my fascination—was growing, as it did now with an awareness of his body next to mine.

"You didn't feel anything for her?" I asked.

"Oh?" He lay back, leaning forward to assess his body, stretching, tensing; and he glanced over at me, a long glance, up and down. I was sure I had seen him do that. I stretched my own body to outmatch his exhibition.

"Of course, my alimony, which I earned, was guaranteed," he went on; "the art I had coached her to buy, the best. I had helped her triple her wealth, beyond what the old titan gave her—he kept her a stupid child." As if this would be an inconsequential occurrence, he said, "She may come to the island this season; I never know where she is. I think in Brazil."

Heat rained down on us. It burst through the thickness of the trees—the sun had pursued us even when we had moved from the sundeck to the lawn, lying down in a shaded patch already invaded by the sun.

"If you ever choose to write about any of this, how will you present it?" he shifted. He had asked that casually as if not committing himself to a suggestion, as if the question was not allowed by his vanity. But he had exposed himself to this:

"If I did, ever, choose to do so—and, really, I doubt it"—I was aiming at his compromised vanity—"do you mean how would I depict you?"

"Of course that's what I meant,' he said, smiling at being caught in an unexpected evasion.

What an opportunity I had to aim at him, to bring him down. "I think I might cast you as a kind of 'Daemon' who invites guests into his lair."

"As asserted by the old horror movies you must have seen and admired, right?—at the Texas Grand Movie Theater in El Paso?" he taunted me. "And the guests accept—"

"Yes." And I knew what was coming.

"—willingly?"

The son of a bitch had cornered me.

"And here you are."

"Yeah, here I am, but in the horror movies that I learned everything from, there was always at least one person who comes to—"

"Confront?"

"Yeah, that. You must have seen the same horror movies I did, man." It was a draw. But his words had stung. I regretted this incursion, regretted his easy rebuttals, his challenging, ironic remarks.

"The subject of evil—does it fascinate you?"

"Yes, and it does you," I said. "I saw the book you left open in the library, and quoted from."

He frowned. "The book—?"

"*The Origin of Evil.* On the library table—with passages marked—the first day you showed me the library."

"I didn't leave any book open. That breaks the spine."

Darkness had thickened. Nebulous forms twisted on the lake, jagged misty silhouettes as we sat on the deck drinking wine, having returned from the lawn to shower and eat a hasty dinner.

He continued where we had left off: "The guest who accepts an invitation in order to confront, would that be you?" he asked. "Or Sonya?" he added when he saw her approaching us.

"Confront what?" Sonya asked. She had walked onto the deck. She was wearing the lightest purple caftan. Occasional gusts of humid wind pasted the material to her body so that she was a nude apparition in the twilight.

"To confront evil," Paul said. "Isn't that what you meant, John?"

"What else . . . man? I learned that from the movies that taught me all I know about writing."

"If you ever write about us"—Sonya joined us, echoing Paul's question—"please, John"—drinking from a glass of wine she had been sipping—"if you do"—until Paul reached up and took it from her, exchanging his for hers, toasting toward the lake—"please don't make me a victim."

"But you are a victim, beauty," Paul said, reaching out to her, drawing her roughly to him.

"I am not. How would you make me that, Paul? How?" She didn't wrest herself away from him, as I had hoped she would.

"Oh, beauty, aren't you, really, that already?" he persisted.

"No." She still did not pull away from him. He drew her face against his, to kiss—no, to—

"Don't!" Sonya protested. He did not release her, until she turned her face away from him sharply. She touched her neck, looked at her hand, licked a finger. "You bit me," she said angrily.

He let her go. "I was in the thrall of my earlier conversation with John—and of course always in the thrall of your glorious beauty."

She moved toward me.

"And, beauty, have you forgotten that you told me that on that runway when I first saw you—and felt the pull of your power"—he pretended to shiver at the memory—"you said, you told me, beauty, that you felt that I had bought you at an auction?"

"I do remember, Paul. My dear beautiful, cruel man, I remember everything." Mimicking his emphatic tone, she added, "Yes, I remember *everything*."

"And me? Me!" Stanty shouted, running in from the dark edge of the deck. He took the glass of wine from Paul and tipped it, but it was now empty. "What about me, John Rechy, what would you write about me?"

"I'd have to wait and see. Maybe you'll do something exceptional that I can write about."

"He will," said Paul.

16

Yesterday—or the day before; it might have been two, even three, days ago, or longer; time drifts by without demarcation— Paul had left off his narrative at an especially tantalizing point. He had bragged that I might not believe how he had overcome what he saw as the most powerful barrier to his ensuring that he would become a rich man—"a very rich man"—when he divorced Corina, "which is what I had planned when I married her."

"You bastard," I said.

"Yes," he accepted that as a compliment. He continued: "I had to leave her grateful—she had to be my ally, forcefully, against her tyrannical father. Otherwise he'd pursue me through the courts. And beyond."

We were sitting at the large table in the dining room, having breakfast, eating fresh fruit—he, a reddish fig he was carefully peeling, holding out a piece of it to me on the tip of his knife, and I took it. Would the son of a bitch leave the story there, yet again?—in order to force me to reveal my interest in it? Or was he coaxing me to break the silence and tell him about my own life in the area—the arena—that aroused his interest, my life on the streets? I wouldn't budge, either way. He served himself a bowl of assorted chilled fruit, blueberries, and strawberries dripping their scarlet juice like drops of pale blood on the table. Even the narrating of our lives had become competitive. His tactic to engage me at his will angered me, and I wanted to let him know that. I stood up. "I'll see you later, Paul." Just that, leaving him at the dining table, alone, and looking—I was glad to note—surprised.

His sudden laughter—at himself, I hoped—followed me out.

Outside, I stood looking about the vast lawn. Noon—it was now noon—had come so quickly, retaining the barest coolness that I knew would not last. I could detect no movement on the other island—I found myself looking toward it, against my intentions. No signal that it was for sale; it was left to the shadows that were crawling over it—that impression survived even though it was a bright, heated day now. Only Stanty claimed to have gone near that island. Had he spread that in the village? The woman there had asked whether "the kid" was still here, "talking stuff."

Each time I sought out the desolate island—from different directions, as I was doing now—it seemed to shun the light. That looming specter of an island, a cold, black presence under the hot livid sun, created in me an insistent sense that violence was buried there.

I cherished my hours in the library, each time marveling at the breadth of Paul's collection of books. I had decided that I would not attempt to read any book I had not read before. The island did not invite commitment to a new book. The involvement with the others on the island was demanding. I would pick out a book that I had read, and would reread favorite passages, or new ones that I came upon.

How quickly and dramatically my life had changed: from the hustling and cruising streets and bars of Los Angeles to this private island, where I could return to an earlier phase in my life, when I would often read two books at once. An invitation and an airplane ticket had accomplished that astonishing change back to that earlier time.

Leaving the library with the book I had chosen to reread in my room, Melville's *Billy Budd*—about a boy's destructive innocence—I ran into one of the gray couple, the woman. Waiting for her, the man was a slice of a shadow against the shaft of light at the top of the stairway. I said, "Good morning" to the woman and received only a disguised nod in response. She hurried up the steps to join the man. He has an odd way of seeming to be hiding or protecting something in one hand, which he keeps somewhat behind him or in his pocket. I would assume that both the man and the woman are mute except that I heard them talking to each other, whispery voices.

I've determined that they tend to the house, although I've never seen them performing any of the various chores which the house requires and are fulfilled. The two might disappear into the night in a motorboat, and reappear invisibly. They might live away from the island or have quarters in this large house. Wherever they dwell, they are like figures created by the shadows in the garden, or like the iron statues that had greeted me my first day on the island, as if those twisted forms had come to life.

17

In my room to leave the book I had chosen before joining whoever would be on the sundeck, I heard the usual bantering and laughter from the lake. Stanty and Sonya swimming, racing each other in the water. I heard Stanty shouting, "I won, I won!" Of course, Sonya would let him claim victory.

Out of one of the speakers situated about the island came waves of music: Stravinsky's *Rite of Spring*, whose cacophonous strains pursued me across the lawn and onto the sundeck, where I joined Paul and Sonya, she still wet from her swim and drinking rum and Coca-Cola—a "Cuba libre," Paul said—fixed by him, refreshed with ice from the bar at the rear of the sundeck. He fixed another of the icy drinks and handed it to me.

Before I could lie on my own pad, Paul sprang up without a word and rushed back toward the house. The music was throttled; it shrieked in protest as if severed with a knife.

"It was too loud," Paul said, lying back down on the deck beside Sonya. "I wouldn't be able to hear Stanty if he called.

Yesterday, he got a cramp in his leg when we were swimming. Of course, he's in superb shape, and he kept on going. Sometimes he overexerts himself."

Difficult to think of Stanty hurting. He was always swimming or rowing, and if alone, far, far off, supposedly toward the unoccupied island—to return with a new exaggeration.

Under the glare of the sun, our bodies were bronzed and shimmering, sensual flesh splayed out together.

Sonya had been moodily recalling a time when she was a girl and her town was constantly in political and violent turmoil. "My father was so afraid for me and my sisters that he taught us how to fire a gun. I hated that time."

I was startled. So much intimacy on this island, and yet I knew so little about her. "I hated the time when I was a soldier, in the infantry," I said, trying to lessen her mood by sharing it.

Paul said to Sonya, "But, beauty, you never know—do you?—when such knowledge might be appropriate. After all, we are on an island, largely unprotected, and there's the other island, and you are, you know, delicious bait."

Though inappropriately jocular—no real menace suggested—he had once again voiced the intimation of something terrible having occurred on the neighboring island.

"Besides, beauty," Paul went on, "you did agree to teach Stanty how to fire a weapon and he—"

"I did not," Sonya interrupted. "I told him I didn't even have a gun. He said that you did." There was a note of disapproval in her voice.

"Oh," Paul said, his punctuation to end a subject.

Sonya got up with Paul's glass and hers to replenish them at the bar. I followed to help her while Paul remained lying down, his eyes shielded by dark sunglasses.

At the bar, as I scooped ice for the glasses, Sonya continued, this time about being "discovered" by the notorious fashion designer Arvayon.

"In the line on the runway. I went to the highest bidder."

She had surprised me by having raised her voice, this time emphatically for Paul to hear. Without sitting up, without removing his sunglasses, Paul called out:

"There was no competition at all."

Silent moments stirred my apprehension of what might be said next, and by whom.

It was Paul:

"Beauty, will you ever regret my choice?" came the voice of the man behind the sunglasses.

And then Sonya:

"I will not. But will you, Paul, ever? Will you ever regret your choice?"

"Oh, beauty."

As if the earlier matter had been festering, Sonya persisted: "I don't know why Stanty would ask me to teach him to fire a weapon when he might have asked you, an expert."

"Of course," Paul refused to be engaged.

"*You* teach him if you want him to learn."

"Of course, beauty. Yes." He sat up. "Beauty, come here," he ordered Sonya when we returned to our pads, the drinks spilling. "I'm craving you, beauty."

She gave herself to him, to another of the violent kisses that I preferred not to witness, resenting his brazen performance. I stared away When I turned around, Sonya had retreated from Paul and was lying next to me.

I was glad Stanty wasn't here to see my avoidance; he would misinterpret my intent. He was probably secretly nearby, ready to spring out . . .

Like now. "Does anybody know I'm here?"

Sonya said, "How could anyone possibly miss knowing that you're here, my darling?"

I never would be able to predict Stanty's reactions. He laughed. "That's good, Sonya; that was really funny."

I had cooled off his obsessive, possessive desire to announce the "blue hour," and there would be no such interval tonight, I knew, as we sat on the deck after dinner. A jagged layer of dark clouds had settled like a ripped shroud over the end of the lake, turning the night deeply dark.

Stanty stood staring ahead at the silent water and the unchanging light, waiting as if something precious that belonged to him had been seized away; and he said—whispered, and only I heard him—he said:

"I wish . . ."

18

In the library, I no longer looked for the book that had attracted
me and had disappeared. On a small table near the stairs there
was, I had noticed, a portable typewriter. I would ask Paul
whether I might keep it in my room. (I did ask him, and he,
of course, said yes.)

Along the hallway, there was another door into what I
thought might be used as a storage room. I had expected it to
be locked, but it wasn't. Looking around, I found some paper
on one of several shelves. I noticed a black metallic box, like
a large, tall safe. Where the statues had been secured that first
night? Where the gun Sonya had referred to was kept locked?

I took the paper and the typewriter to my room. Covering with a dry towel, at least for now, the dizzy painting, I sat
down; rolled paper into the typewriter, which was surprisingly
new; and I wrote:

*A letter came through the offices of Grove Press in New
York, forwarded to me in Los Angeles, where I lived in a
room in a downtown hotel on Hope Street. The letter was
from a man responding in admiration to two stories I had*

written, recently published. "Mardi Gras" had recounted,
as closely as I could remember out of the fog of hallucina-
tion, what I thought of now as my season in hell, when,
during the Mardi Gras carnival in New Orleans, drunk
and drugged and sleepless for sex-driven nights and days,
I saw leering clowns on gaudy floats tossing cheap neck-
laces to grasping hands that clutched and grabbed and tore
them, spilling beads; and revelers crawled on littered streets,
wrestling for them, bleeding for them—and beads fell on
spattered blood like dirty tears—and I saw costumed revel-
ers turn into angels, angels into demons, demons into clown-
ing angels; and in a flashing moment the night split open
into a deeper, darker chasm out of which soared demonic
clowning angels laughing.

During the purging of Ash Wednesday, as the mourn-
ing bells of St. Louis Cathedral tolled, the withering grass of
Jackson Square nearby became a battleground of bodies, of
men and women besotted with liquor and pills and drugs,
passed out like corpses under a frozen white sun; and I fled
the hellish city.

I pulled the page out and started to crumple it. I had no
intention of continuing what I had begun to write—even the
memory pitched me back into those hellish days.

I put the typed sheet under my clothes in a drawer.

After a brief interval of moderate surcease from the heat—a layer
of clouds had intercepted the ferocious sun—the heat returned
more intense as if it had withdrawn to gain more power.

Overnight, two or three large electric fans had appeared in the house, one in the library, another in the large living room. I assumed they had been picked up in the village by the somber gray couple.

In the library now, even the insistent whirring of the fan was welcome, proof that the heat was in relative check.

I was relieved, when I entered the library, to find that Stanty was not there, and glad when Paul followed me in. We sat at the long table surrounded by shelves of books.

I had adhered to my determination not to prod him to continue where he had left off his account of his marriage to Corina and his cunning guarantee of his fortune.

"And among your more literary influences?"

He hoarded subjects, readied in his mind to be continued without a break. I wouldn't indicate that he still startled me. I'd move on to challenge him, past his sarcasm about "literary" influences, and I would confound him by mentioning three writers, all women, one of whom I was sure he would not recognize—and I relied on that.

The easy one. "Djuna Barnes."

"A dark jungle of words," he identified her, approving. "And—?"

"Kathleen Winsor."

"Her trash influenced you?"

I sensed an ambush on my intention to baffle him with a name unfamiliar to him, but I also felt annoyance at his reference to *Forever Amber* as trash. I had learned about that novel in El Paso after dutiful Sunday Mass in the Church of the Immaculate Conception when I was fourteen. The sickly priest led the congregation in a vow never to read books forbidden by the Church. Most emphatically he mentioned *Forever*

Amber—"an affront to all morality, a base, lurid exhibition that flies in the face of our Lord." I stole it from a book and record shop, carrying it out among my schoolbooks. (The owner of the shop later told me she'd seen me take it but ignored the theft because she had been thrilled to see a boy stealing a book.)

"No, man, not trash at all," I defended that favorite book. "It's written in Technicolor prose, and I learned that's good sometimes, and other times only black-and-white prose, like in Kafka, no colors." That was true; in my description of the Mardi Gras carnival I had attempted such effects—the garish carnival, the somber cemetery of drunk revelers.

"Who else?"

I'd catch him on this one. "—Aphra Behn."

"A spy and a writer—sixteen-hundreds, no? She influenced you?"

Son of a bitch. "Yes," I said. In college I had encountered her and had been attracted to her melodramatic and suggestive novels of intrigue; she used some of the same plots Shakespeare dramatized—with entirely different results.

"Sartre, Aphra Behn, Camus, and Winsor and, of course, Shakespeare?" Paul listed. "A formidable group of influences. Of course," he added in a voice that alerted me to a taunt, "Camus exists only until you reach—what age?—puberty?"

"What a fucken cliché, Paul. Where'd you hear that? I'm sure you'll add that Sartre takes over."

"Sartre does."

He angered me with his implicit dismissal of a favorite book. "*The Stranger*—"

"Because—?" He interrupted me.

"In plain prose, it affirms the banality of fate." Okay, if that sounded stilted.

"Of course. In enumerating your influences"—he was determined—"I omitted algebraic progressions in dogged pursuit of that evasive mysterious X."

I corrected him: "Algebraic equations."

His strategy shifted: "You use real people as your characters?" Again avoiding the obvious, a possible reference to himself as a subject.

I met his stare. "Yeah, reflections of them, my view, as fairly as possible."

"Do you include yourself in that epic sweep of fairness?" He smiled at his own sarcasm, which I ignored.

"As an imitation, with some similarities. It's tempting to paint even that imitation in flattering hues. I resist that to the point of inventing some terrible things so I'll be praised for my honesty." I didn't wait for him to slice into that. "And your influences, Paul?"

"No one, nothing," he said.

Although he seemed serious, I said, "Come on, man, that's bullshit."

"All right, one," he bartered. "Can you guess?"

"Ayn Rand." I held my breath. I had intended to bait him, reduce some of his thinking to its most superficial, the very least, a parody of thinking—but if he said yes?

"That dumb creature? Come on, you can't believe—"

"No, I didn't," I confessed, in relief.

"Writers whose lives or works explore—even champion—violence," he said, "and who redefine good and evil: Genet, Beckett, Baudelaire, Mishima. Violence as purification: Nietzsche, and—yes—Swift, and Henry Miller—"

"Whom I dislike," I interjected.

"Miller's libertarian—libertine—philosophy?—you dislike? Surely not."

"I dislike his dirty sexuality."

"*You?*" he accused.

"Yeah. Sex in Henry Miller is dirty because the partici-pants are ugly and dirty." I would try to deflect what I suspected might have been coming, a further dissertation on the purgative of violence and evil. "You know what makes a really hot, sexy scene in a book, man?"

"Yes?"

"At least one of the participants in any sexual configuration—at least one of the players, or of course more, or, best, all of them—must be beautiful and sexy." If I was to divert what I had interrupted, I might be bolder: I might court his vanity. "If I ever write about this island—"

"Yes?" I was succeeding; he was interested. "And—?"

"I'll describe everyone as beautiful: Sonya—"

"That's easy. And Stanty. My son is beautiful. And?"

I waited, silent. I thought I heard footsteps—Stanty, lurking—but it was a sound that came from the whirling fan.

"And?"

"Of course, you, man. You'll be—"

"Sensational? Like you," he guaranteed the compliment by extending it to me. He stretched his body—that recurring tendency goaded by justifiable vanity.

We were lying on mats on the sundeck, drinking the chilly Cuba libres that he had just made at the bar and which he had become especially fond of. We had left the library when gray clouds ambushed the harsh sun, a signal that the sundeck was a viable location now, in filtered light.

"Céline, Sade—" he resumed. "The 'saints' of our time, the demons, the heroes of all who look into the maw of existence and see only corruption and ugliness."

"I don't understand you, Paul," I ventured. "You contradict yourself constantly, and sometimes when you talk, what you say sounds really good—deep, man—but it doesn't make sense." My anger surprised me.

It didn't displease him. "In a world full of contradictions, is that all you don't understand? Me?"

"That's pretty arrogant, to assume you're the only object of mystery."

"You like to solve mysteries?"

"Some mysteries shouldn't be solved; they should be left mysterious. I'd bet this didn't happen, that it's apocryphal—and I prefer apocryphal claims—"

"Because—?"

"An anecdote waits to find the proper person to attach to—like that Alice Toklas asked Gertrude Stein—at Stein's deathbed, no less—asked her: 'What is the answer?' and Stein answered, 'What is the question?' And, man, that was her *answer*, man; the perfectly understood question *is* the answer." I paused. I was breathless, like a damn student, damn it—okay, a bright student.

I anticipated a readied rebuttal.

"It's so damn hot," he said.

"You're a son of a bitch, man," I said, smarting at being dismissed so rudely.

"Anyone else you don't understand?" he asked.

"Yeah. Stanty. You seem to encourage him to be—" This was my opportunity to trump him with ridicule.

"To be?" His voice was serious.

I would do it, shift his interest to absurdity, yet leave the actual matter of the puzzling relationship pending. "You seem to encourage him to be—"

"Yes?"

"—naughty."

"Naughty!" He threw his head back and laughed. "Stanty? Naughty? I won't even conjecture what he would do if he thought anyone had called him 'naughty.'"

"I'd tell him I was . . . joshing."

"Good, man, good." He was grading our repartee, a draw.

But I had entered mined territory. "You seem to be studying Stanty."

As if to organize his thoughts, he reached for the pack of cigarettes he still carried. He patted the package, allowing the filter of a cigarette to protrude. He put the chosen cigarette between his lips. He returned it to the pack. "My son," he said in a soft voice, each word pronounced clearly. "Stanty—" He was not looking at me. "My son Stanty—I'm in awe of him, I watch him becoming what I—who he will be." He shook his head as if negating what he had allowed. He pulled the rejected cigarette out, lit it, and puffed deeply, holding the smoke. He exhaled, long. "Stanty," he said, and surprised me: "Constantine."

"I don't understand what you said."

"I didn't intend you to."

Yet what he had said—I would try to remember it, find clues in the scrambled words. I tried to resume: "I understand Sonya."

"What if she surprises you?" he added, with grave seriousness. "What if under the extravagant beauty there's someone you don't know at all, cunning under the facade of beauty? Perhaps an undecided conspirator?"

He was attempting to taint my feelings for Sonya. Implying that she and he might be secret allies? Not Sonya, not Sonya, who had balked at showing Stanty how to shoot.

He moved closer to me as we lay on the lawn on the towels we had carried from the sundeck, he leaned toward me as if to convey something of enormous gravity that must be kept close, and quiet, delivered softly, something perhaps read and memorized.

"The only way to conquer cruelty is with more cruelty, not with what is called 'good.' No, only two equally powerful forces, not a weak one against a powerful one—no contest. Not good against evil—no contest—but evil against evil." He paused as if to gauge his own words. His tone changed: "I'll be surprised if you don't agree, man," he said, "since you see a world ruled by your clowning angels, groveling for tossed glass beads or filthy money on dirty streets."

An image he had retained from my story; a connection made to his.

Through his tirades—we were sitting on the deck drinking wine and staring into a starless steamy night—I listened, even at times when what he said, or implied, repelled me. Though blurred—his recurring deliberate camouflage?—what he had said might evolve into a frightening philosophy. At times he lost me in a crush of words, words mouthed for effect, to challenge, never intending to act on their implications. Despite those probationary deductions, I felt angry now at the contempt he expressed, the justification of all he did. I rummaged to rebut him, but all I can come up with is this withheld question about his motives: "In your marriages . . . Paul . . . did anything definite trigger your angry separations?"

He looked at me as if baffled that an answer so obvious should have been questioned. He shrugged and said: "It was time."

"Have you ever felt cruel, Paul?"

"No."

19

Paul, Sonya, and I are sitting on stools at the bar on the sundeck under the shade of the canopy, which does little to check the heat. I glance down at our intertwined bare legs, Sonya's—she's in the middle—are smooth, lighter-dark, curling toward Paul's, much darker, and then, turning on the stool to brush against mine, darker still, exposed flesh that darkens or lightens and glows with our shifting motions.

Sonya had removed the top of her suit, displaying bold nipples glistening with drops of perspiration that lingered until—this is happening now—Paul leans over and dabs them away with one flick of his tongue on each.

I relish the physical resplendence on the island: When Sonya wanders moodily about the lawn—which has miraculously survived the scorching sun—she looks like a golden ghost, lost within the shifting shade of trees. Paul, darker every day—I note this now—is leaner, more defined, his long muscles carved into his body. (In a glance, I notice that his trunks—sweat nestling at his groin—reveal his endowment, but, then, he just licked Sonya's breasts. I won't allow him to note my competition; I put on my sunglasses, and face away.) I am more

muscular than he, more defined than when I first arrived. (I
work out in a section of the boathouse that I converted into
an adequate gym, with chairs and bracing bars; I caught Stanty
there one day, working out. "Good," I said; that was all.) I have
succeeded in turning darker than Paul by going to the sundeck
alone when they're all swimming. I can't honestly avoid Stanty
in my evaluation. His hair has turned streaked blond, his flesh
is coffee-colored—I notice that as he runs onto the sundeck.

"Sonya wanted to swim to the other island today," he
announced.

Sonya protested, in her warm tone, "It was you who suggested it, my darling, and I said it was too far to swim, remember?" She had quickly covered her breasts when Stanty burst in.

We are still at the bar sipping Paul's refreshed Cuba libres.

Stanty dismissed, "I forgot. . . . You know, John Rechy, I'm
the only one who's ever been even near the other island. Ask
my father, he'll tell you."

"That's right," Paul said—acquiesced, I thought.

"I swam there today," Stanty announced.

Sonya corrected him gently: "You didn't swim there, my
sweet—"

"I did, I—"

"—you rowed there," Sonya said.

"Same thing. I could have swum." He grabbed a hand-
ful of ice and pushed it into his mouth. When it had melted,
he went on breathlessly: "Listen to this, everyone: There was
a man at an upstairs window in the house on that island, he
yelled something angry at me. I couldn't hear him, he was too
far away."

The house I thought I had discerned—was it really there?
I anticipated Stanty's fearful twists, which came:

"He said if I ever came around, he'd shoot me."

No reaction of alarm from Sonya or Paul.

"But you said you couldn't hear him," I said.

"This is how it happened: When the man was at the window, he knew I couldn't hear him; so he shouted at me, and that's when I was able to hear him. That's when he threatened to kill *any*one he caught there, and he meant it." Having delivered his fearful news, and as if to avoid any further interrogation, he walked away.

Perhaps there was a caretaker on the grounds now. Someone else? I caught myself; I was lending credence to Stanty's fantasies. There was nothing living on that island. The condition of what had been verdure and remained—browning leaves, broken branches, bare trunks—indicated, even from afar, a desolation that precluded life. As to a window: Out of the mushy murk, only once had I even imagined—the impression had vanished instantly—the existence of a house, and that had been, I saw as I stared, just a skeletal outline amid collapsed, dark, rotting rubble, perhaps the remains of what was once a house. Stanty had invented a window in order to locate a threatening intruder, and he— Jesus Christ! Why was he now demanding to learn to fire a gun?

20

At the desk in my bedroom, I reached for the page I had typed before. What I had written sounded like an opening to a story about the island. I had no intention of writing such a thing. I have no idea how such an account, if written, would end; and I believe that an ending must have retrospective inevitability, everything leading to it along the way, fate found only in retrospect; and if I did ever write about this island—but I won't, I know that—how would I fulfill my own requirement of inevitable fate? Dredge up Stanty's hostility leading to . . . ? Sonya: plant terrible hints that she may betray . . . ? No, no, not her. Paul: the contradictions, the implicit championing of violence that would . . . All—everything—would have to conclude in an eruption of . . . quiet violence, explosive violence? And the mysterious island festering with . . . ? All useless considerations. I will never write about this island.

In the library earlier, I had looked for, but not found, a collection that included Shirley Jackson's "The Lottery." Into the seeming banality of the early pages, she had woven intimations, in the very prose, of the inevitability of the violence. But where are events on this island moving? Everything evolves unexpectedly, and then is forgotten, ignored, relegated to silence.

Clouds are massing outside my window. They're rent apart in the distance by flashing bolts of lightning followed by moans of thunder. The moisture in the air is thick; the heated lake adds its own moisture. The colors of the intrusive painting seem to swirl about the room.

I sit before the typewriter and write:

He was still gazing in the direction of the darkened island; quietly as if speaking out his thoughts, and almost—and this occurred to me quickly—as if quoting memorized words, he said: "What happens to evil when its flames are snuffed? Does it wait to spring out?" He had been gazing at the shadowed island when he said that.

I took the typed page out. About to rip it and the earlier page into pieces so no one else might read them, I stopped. I put them back in the drawer.

21

To allow an easier flow to the slightest breeze from the lake, I had left the door of my bedroom open. In my jockey shorts, I sit up in my bed, reading the book I took earlier from the library, an old favorite I first read in school, *Don Quixote*. The real battle, between the author and his character, continued to fascinate me: a modern novel written centuries ago; the author as antagonist.

I hear the footsteps that usually go past my door. They do not continue on. I see a distinct form where the door is ajar.

"May I come in?" It's Paul.

"Sure, come in," I said.

He's in his undershorts—white jockeys, a bold contrast to his tanned body. I am intently aware of his near-nudity and conscious of my own. It's so hot that the temperature demands the least clothing, and he probably just left Sonya's bedroom. Not wanting to call attention to my action, I don't raise the sheet over my body. When that would become less obvious, I will cover myself more fully, although—in these confused moments—I'm not sure about the reason for my reactions, since Paul and I lie on the deck sunning in trunks virtually every day.

He does not seem self-conscious, and I relax.

But I tense when, instead of sitting on one of the chairs in the room, he sits on my bed, easily, without a word. He lies beside me, head to feet.

Looking out the wide window, I see bolts of lightning stabbing the night. In sputtering instants of flashing light, the room is like one in an old black-and-white movie when the film breaks and light proceeds to snap.

"I hate women," Paul announces; "I detest them. They're fucken whores, bitches, cunts."

"You don't mean it," I say quickly.

He seems not to have heard me.

"I just left Sonya. We fucked, I desire her, her body drives me crazy and I hate her for that and I wish I didn't need her or her body. I desire—no, I need her—and hate her but more than anything else I need her for me to despise. I hate all the fucken bitches I've fucked, and I'll continue to desire them and fuck them and hate them before I need them again, and that's what keeps me theirs and drives me mad."

My instinct is to rebut his hateful burst of words, to refuse to listen to him; but his rant causes me to wait to see how far it would go, whether it would retrench, disclaim itself. My feeling toward Sonya, a friendship that is becoming increasingly close, confuses me. At times I feel that I'm sexually attracted to her, but then I dismiss that thought. It has to do with the competition between me and Paul.

In my bedroom on this island, that fierce hot sweaty night—no breath of a lost breeze recurred—I had become keenly aware of Paul's body next to mine. If he was attempting to display his body, then I would display my own. I won't, as I had earlier determined to do, cover my own almost-nudity.

"I mean it, man," he had just said. "I lust after women, love and hate them, I need to fuck them until they're exhausted and I'm exhausted. It's lust that drives me to them, man, and desire—needing them—lessens me. Need is humiliating."

There was no detectable irony in his venomous declaration. He meant it all. There was evidence in the way he ordered Sonya to him—and in the violent connection that followed, a feral kiss.

"I'm surprised you even used the word 'love,' man," I said, thinking that this might intercept the violent rush.

"Love is the same as hate," he said.

"Come on, man, that's a cliché, not good enough for you." I wanted to introduce the possibility of rebuttal, add lightness to the uncomfortable declaration. "It sounds good, man, everybody says it, but it doesn't make sense."

"The same intensity, the same, the same"—thrusting out the next word with disgust—"*need*."

"Love can fuck up desire, I'll agree to that," I said, and I believed that. If, on the occasions when someone I had sex with remained after orgasm, and an edge of friendship was being suggested to me—as, say, we might lie, though rarely, talking—if, then, at those times, all desire faded. The slightest intimation of affection ruled out the possibility of further sexual contact. I sought out strangers, strangers who would be defined only by the sexuality involved: no names exchanged; no possibility other than accidental contact, still anonymous, unrecognized, recurring perhaps in an alley; recognizing whoever I was with, if at all, only when we parted.

In the room with Paul, what remained of the light—I had pushed away the reading lamp—glowed only faintly. The air was stilled, a presence bearing down on our bodies.

"That bitch Corina"—Paul went on—"that lying hypo-crite. Her life had been all girls' schools with spectral nuns. With her family, she'd had private audiences with priests, bish-ops, cardinals—her family, equal hypocrites, bought them all, including a private audience with the fucken pope. Even after we were married, she went to Mass every Sunday; she would rush into whatever church she saw, kneel, praying. At times, I would go with her—you know why, man?—to watch her be ridiculous. I could belittle her more for that, and I did. I would have her kneel before me like she did in those churches, and I would make her beg to get fucked. Then she'd go to confession.

" 'What do you confess to?' I asked her.

" 'Lust,' she said; 'lust is sinful.'

"She would say that as she reached over to me, pushing her body against mine, unbuttoning my pants and raising her dress, pulling my cock out, shoving it into her." His hand dropped to his groin, cupping it over the white shorts in recollection of those frenzied contacts. In a glance, I saw once again—but, this time, it was much more emphatic—the assertive mound between his legs, lingering, of course, from his contact earlier with Sonya.

I placed my own hand between my legs, over the sheet, matching him, and listening.

"And she was fucken frigid all that time," he said.

He leaned over his side of the bed, where he had placed his cigarettes. He took one out and lit it, this time without sheltering it. Even the tip of flame seemed to add to the heat. A pause, while he inhaled, deep, holding the smoke, releasing it, a small swirl rising into the heat. Without puffing on it again, he ground the cigarette on the palm of his hand. He leaned back beside me.

"Man, I had to have her as an ally against her father, and I knew how. Listen:

"Outside Paris, there was an old church we had driven by before, one she said she loved. She had rushed in for penance, left some money, as she did at every goddamn church she went to. I suspected she was praying to the saints for an orgasm." He paused to laugh. "The church was an ancient country church, the kind named after some saint or other who someone claimed performed some ridiculous miracle and, with vast humility, man"—he laughed at that—"asked for a church in his name. It was a church with gaudy statues, an array of goddamned anonymous saints, a tableau of bloody processions—and Jesus, naked on the cross."

I knew what he was describing. Even as a child, I had been awed by the painted statues of saints and angels and suffering martyrs, especially Jesus on the cross, the nudity of the perfect, muscular body so startling among robed, kneeling mourners, and men enclosed in armor.

"Before we entered the church"—Paul was now leaning on his elbow, talking—"she paused, transfixed by this ancient church, just one of many that had helped to render her frigid, driven her frenzied needs and left her unfulfilled, demanding more and more, draining. Inside, she dipped her manicured fingers into the bowl of filthy water, and, kneeling, she crossed herself."

And I was swept into the long-withheld, now vivid story. I imagined the scene. The mournful reverence in church, the spectacle of women depicted in paintings and statuary, always covered in gray or black, and always weeping glass tears. All amid the spectrum of colors, of stained-glass windows lit by the afternoon sun, creating dyed pools, filtered reflections of colors melting on the floor, candles radiating in stifled silence, an atmosphere of fear and mourning and death—and smashed sexuality. All of it in tawdry Technicolor.

Lighting another cigarette, snuffing it out on his palm, Paul continued: "Scattered about were two—no, three—people, kneeling; two were women, their heads draped with black shawls, their busy fingers roaming over strung beads, muttering prayers, hurling them out like muted curses, and an old man with a cane, all worn bones, trying to kneel, head bowed before the golden altar."

Beside me, Paul had lain back, his eyes closed as he painted the remembered scene.

"To one side of the church, inside, there was an alcove I had noticed the first time with her here, an alcove ruled by a large statue of Jesus on the cross, and of course naked except for that band of cloth, barely covering his groin, a long, long piece of cloth suggesting the size of what it hid. In the glow of flickering candles, the figure before us seemed to be breathing, a witness to Corina's outrageous beauty, which she was displaying before the posing naked man in this old temple of repression and martyrdom and festering sex."

Paul's voice grew husky, his words rushed: "I grabbed Corina, I pushed her roughly down in front of the commanding naked figure, she needed no coaxing, she knelt, pleading wordlessly, I coaxed her down, pushing her to the floor, she sprawled there, she growled, a sound of stifled laughter, her mouth open in choked silence—all twisted and thrilling—and I laughed and I pulled at her clothes, tearing, welcoming the sound of violent ripping, and she laughed, her laughter thrust into the deadly silence, and she spread her naked legs open, I pushed my pants down, I mounted her, she thrust her body up to hasten and then to deepen the penetration, I pushed into her, hard, I fucked her hard, harder, hard, and we laughed, man."

I closed my eyes, images of naked flesh exploding in blinding colors.

Paul's voice thickened, deep, guttural: "I fucked her, and she was moaning, and her groans fought the silence, destroyed it. The scattering of people there looked around, alarmed. The old man attempted to get up from the pew he had leaned into; he moved forward toward where sounds were coming, his cane wobbled, and he fell not far from where we lay on the floor fucking, my cock buried in her cunt, throbbing, pushing deeper and out, deeper. The panting old man grasped his cane and tried to rise, succeeding finally and staggering toward us, his mouth open, making soundless gasps.

"'What are——?' the old man managed to utter. 'Are you——?' He was unable to finish. One of the women had followed him; her thick black shawl fell off her head, tangling at her feet. She grasped for it, chanting. '*Dios mio, dios mio,*' she pleaded in Spanish. In Spanish, man, she pleaded in *Spanish.*"

I saw it all, the beautiful woman Corina, her white legs wide open, the man's hands spreading them wider, his buttocks pumping down on her, and the statue of the naked Jesus, covered only with a cloth that dipped down low at his groin, that naked man straining in pain—oh, no, no, no—straining no longer in pain but in passion, released and straining in passion, staring down at them, as if about to descend to join the bodies exposed by the burned light of candles and sun-filtered colors bleeding on the floor.

Beside me on the bed, Paul laughed, trying to speak more words through gasps of laughter in this hot room, heat from our bodies coiling into it. He blurted: "I saw the pious man and the woman staring at us, I fucked the glorious naked body harder, moving our bodies sideways to expose them fully to the watchers, who stood unmoving. Within Corina's moans, I heard the sound of two other congregants who had walked in and were rushing out, screaming, and the one woman watching resumed her chant: '*Dios mio, dios mio!*' In Spanish, man! The two others were running out as if chased by the devil, screaming out their prayers crazily and loud as if to stifle our moans. Yes, screaming their prayers, '*Madre de dios, madre de dios,*'" Paul stuttered between bursts of laughter. "In Spanish," he said. "Praying. In Spanish, man."

It was now as if the laughter in that country church had joined the laughter in this room, and my own choking laughter, spurts of it, controlled, then rushing out beyond control at the lurid, impossible spectacle,

Paul groped his groin firmly. I felt my own cock responding to the daring sacrilege of his story, the spectacular sexual transgression.

"The old man continued to hobble toward us until he was almost over us, and Corina was coming, and staring up, coming for all the times she had not, looking up and screaming yes, yes, yes, in that ancient church, screaming, and she came and came, my lips on her lips, biting her until I tasted blood—" He stopped, catching his breath, stopped the laughter, only to allow more words; and then between gasps of resumed laughter, and sudden surprised silences—his and mine—he said, "And then, man, and then, man, oh, man, then there stood a priest, a young priest in his cassock, and I was holding myself back but not all the way and Corina pushed herself up in rhythmic thrusts and let herself go again and again on and on and she was coming, she was coming, and the young priest shouted something at us, about blasphemy, about police, about sin at the same time that his hands clasped his cassock at his groin and his breathing was loud, louder." Paul shook with more spurts of laughter. "That young priest—his hands clasping his groin!

"And Corina said, man, that bitch with my cock pulsing in her cunt; she said, Corina said, 'Don't stop, fuck me deep, goddammit, don't stop, fuck me, fuck me, let him see us, let him see us—'"

The young priest? The old man who lingered? Or the figure of Christ staring down over them within the anxious glow of mesmerized candles?

I was laughing now with Paul, laughing at the glorious excess.

"'Don't stop, fuck me, don't stop,' Corina gasped, and I didn't, faster, coming, deeper, faster, and she came again, and the young priest gaping down at us said:

"'Oh, God! Oh, *God!*'

"And Corina gasped:

"'*Oh, Jesus Christ!*'"

After minutes of uncontrolled laughter, Paul fell back on the bed. Sweat and tears of laughter stung my eyes. The laughter fading, fading, faded, and we both stopped laughing. Paul turned over on his side, facing me as I faced him.

Then:

There remained in the room only an emptiness, as if all sound, all laughter, all words had coagulated into the heat, a silence louder than laughter, no sound, and then I heard the nervous rustling of trees outside, a gasp of wind shaking their leaves. I waited for the resultant breeze to glide into the room, and it did, brushing over our bodies. Then again only the soundless echo of our laughter.

Paul got up. He stood staring out the window. His silhouette was etched against the vague darkness. Lightning and thunder had brought no rain, had left only its distinct scent, moist, a fading scent.

He turned around to face me.

"I've tried to be a homosexual," he said.

22

Still in bed, the sheet now cast away, I knew I had heard those words distinctly uttered by Paul, facing me.

"How did you do that, Paul?" I asked him.

He turned around, walked back to the edge of the bed. "What?" he asked as if orienting himself to his own words.

"You said you tried to be a homosexual."

He lay back down next to me, head to feet. "I even tried drag."

I laughed, deliberate laughter, loud laughter.

He winced and I tried to compensate: "Trying to picture you in drag—" It was difficult: the defined muscles, his handsome angular face, his masculine manners, his arrogant stride—in drag? "Jesus, Paul, you must have looked ridiculous."

It worked. He laughed, too. "I did look awful, like a man in drag! It was in Paris; I went to a party. Genet was there. He was in drag, too, and he looked like the tough convict he had been—in drag. Someone asked if we were lesbian twins."

I didn't have to force laughter now; it came easily.

"He is a superb writer." Even now, he startled me with his abrupt shifts. "The life he lived, the life he describes—masquerading, living at the edge of despair and danger, in prison for years—"

Even now, a tinge of his sarcasm aimed at my own brief incarceration; and he went on:

"—and exhilaration, danger, a courtship with evil, courting evil, that's living, the life I admire, accepting it all, welcoming it all, a part of it all—"

Courting evil. . . . "In drag?" I tried clumsily to break a new tension aggravated by his words.

"High drag," he said, shifting again. "Dress, high heels, stockings, everything, like the queen in your story, Miss—"

"—Destiny." Miss Destiny, the defiant queen in my story, Miss Destiny, who swore to storm heaven and protest, to confront and judge God. In drag.

Paul's face shone with sweat. "I wanted to feel entirely like a woman, to feel the goddamned power of a woman, to understand why I was bound to them, needed them—wanted to release myself—"

I was welcoming the promiscuous rambling—it kept me from understanding what I wasn't sure I wanted to understand, his casual admiration of evil, a word that lingered in my mind unwanted, floating at the top of his rush of words in this room saturated with sweat, which, evaporating, gave to our bare flesh a welcome coolness.

"But it didn't work, man," he said. "That night, in drag, I fucked two whores, pulling out of one, entering the other, fucking each, back to front to back—and then I began tearing the drag I had kept on, the delicate things, tearing them strip by strip, peeling them away, the women's things as if it was those that bound me." He burst into mean laughter, harsh, rough laughter. "Stripping away those fucken clothes, their clothes, their power, I ordered the sluts to blow me one after the other until I shoved one away, and I kept one to take it all, swallow my cock to my balls, and I pushed her head till my cock was all the way down her fucken throat, and I wanted to feel all sensation gathering there, for me, in me, in my cock, my cock pulsing in her throat, and I forced her head to stay there—deep in her fucken throat, feeling it all, all of it, feeling my cock, man, pulsing, alive, man, my cock, me—until she choked, still I kept her there, shooting spurts of cum into her throat, every drop of my fucken cum in her fucken cunt-mouth."

He lay back, exhausted, next to me. We lay silent, both of us, as if trapped within the frozen heat.

He stood up, staring down at me. His shorts were soaked with sweat, pasted against his groin. He looked naked, the saturated cloth outlining his aroused cock, pushing at the thin white tissue of the shorts.

I looked away from him, looked down at my own body, the sheet matted under me with sweat, my own cock outlined within my shorts, and straining.

After a time whose length I couldn't determine, Paul walked out.

23

When we faced each other, the morning after the sweaty night—which had yielded to a warm coolness this morning—what would either of us say? Would we try to avoid each other? Was there need for embarrassment? It had been the graphic eroticism of his narrative—it was that which had threatened to arouse us both.

Still in bed, I could hear the sounds of Stanty in the water. I got up and looked out the window and saw him bobbing up and down, splashing. With him was Paul, just as exuberant. That meant Sonya would be alone.

Shifting my sight, I saw her through the window. She was walking slowly along the edge of the lake. Her head was lifted slightly back, slightly defiant, I thought.

I put on my pants over my bathing trunks. I hurried to the front of the house. Through the wide window in the living room, I located her as she wound about the lake. Her filmy azure caftan wrapped itself about her body as she walked, and then it drifted away, a misty veil. From this distance, she looked like a specter, pensive, or lost. No longer defiant—sad.

I walked out, hurrying to catch up with her on the lawn.

She turned around. "John!"

"I'm sorry, I don't want to interrupt your walk." I pretended to be moving away, hoping she would respond as she did:

"My darling John, you are not intruding. Join me." Smiling her entrancing smile, she put her arm through mine. A feeling of warmth coursed through me—no, not the heat already conquering the day, the warmth of her flesh.

We walked along the path, silently, until she said:

"I think Paul is going to leave me."

"Sonya." I uttered her name softly, an assurance of trust for whatever she might say. "Why do you think that?"

She looked away from me, as if what she wanted to say might embarrass her. "Paul has always been very—oh, sexual and demanding," she continued. "He likes to 'play games,' as he says. I want to tell you, but—" A long pause, as if she was determining whether to go on.

I thought she might stop, and I believe I hoped so, not wanting to hear what I suspected might be coming.

She weighed her words: "Even when his games became—excessive—even then I knew I could control them, and he allowed that. But, recently, here on the island, the pretense of hostility—yes, that's it—the pretense seems, but only at times, only at times, it seems to be turning real. As if—what?—as if it angers him to desire me, but he does desire me." She added emphatically, "I don't doubt that."

I was sure she would not go on. Instead, as if she had gathered all her determination to speak, she rushed her words: "At times now it's as if he wants to devour me, not stop, to the point of hurting me, frightening me. At times it's as if he wants to become me, banish me so that he can feel twice, what he feels, himself, what I feel—and then what only he feels, needs, wants—and not stopping, not stopping."

What she had been saying—as she slid sideways seeking the edge of a shadow and closer to me as we lay on the lawn, under a fresh shadow the way Stanty had seen us that earlier time, and I hoped he would see us again—about his need for women, his detestation of that need—it confirmed what he had said to me. I had continued to harbor the possibility that she might be an exception. As I voiced the words, I heard their inadequacy: "But the way he kisses you, in front of everyone"—in front of me, drawing her to him, pushing his body against hers as if there, then, he would take her; but all that affirmed what she had said. I had wanted only to assuage her feelings of abandonment. "And he—"

"As a lover—strictly as a lover," she emphasized, "he remains . . . sensational."

"—calls you 'beauty.'" I was fumbling.

She threw her head back with a laugh. "'Beauty!' He began calling me that soon after we met—because he couldn't remember my name." Her laughter almost drowned her words: "After the summer, he's going back to Paris. Always before, he's told me where we're going, even seeming to consult with me. Not now, not this time. Just that he's going. Shall we sit here?" she said after we stood up to avoid the encroaching sun and were passing a bench under the spill of a large shadow. The sun had gained heat, negating the coolish moment, and it had begun to erase the shadow we had found.

WHWACKK!

A shot rang out in the distance.

WHWACKK! WHWACKK! Another, another.

I stood up looking in the direction of the deserted island.

Sonya had remained calm. "It's Paul and Stanty," she said, raising a hand to me to rejoin her on the bench. "He's showing him how to shoot because I wouldn't do it."

"Is the gun available to him?"

"Paul keeps it locked up," she assured me.

Still nervous at the violent intrusion of gunshots, I sat down close to her, listening to the fading sounds of the fired gun until they died.

"If Paul does attempt to discard me," she rushed her words, "I would—" Her face twisted in anger.

Would she say what I thought was forming in her mind?— an intimation of violence aroused by the sound of the fired gun? This extremity of angered love, from this woman whose serenity I had come to admire, and whom, yes, I was coming to love—yes, possibly to love—was it possible that she was capable of what I was sure she had been about to confess?

I would—?

We remained for a longer time under the cooling clutch of low branches we had moved to, away from the pursuit of the sun.

"Island! Island!"

It was Stanty's voice.

"They're celebrating with their intimate signal," Sonya said, then: "Stanty's a sad child."

"I haven't seen that," I said. "He seems overly confident." Yet there had been that haunting moment when he had whispered into the void of the lake:

I wish . . .

"He's frightened—and confused."

The moment seemed right to ask: "Is Corina Stanty's mother?"

"I don't know," she said. "I'm not sure Stanty knows either."

"How the hell is that possible?" Incomprehensible even for what was unwinding on this island.

"He refers to each by her name—the rare times when he mentions them—often with hatred, at times gasped with what might be longing. He seems so unsettled each time that occurs that I have never questioned him. I asked Paul, only once; and he was furious, demanding that I never bring that up—my 'filthy curiosity,' he dismissed it."

"Impossible," I whispered, more to myself. Like the heat rising after deceptive moments of cloudy respite, the ambiguity about Stanty's mother added to the tension that the island itself seemed to conspire to sustain.

"Would you like to have sex with Paul?"

I looked away from her to dismiss her question.

"Would you have sex with me?" she said.

I stared at her beside me, her startling beauty, Paul's mistress. A fleeting image: the body of the man who had lain beside me that sweaty night, him—that supremely confident and arrogant man—and she, Sonya, their naked bodies entangled . . . Compete? Affront him? Would I? Sonya as a prize? No, not her, not Sonya, no. Confused, I blurred my answer: "If so, what would Paul—?"

"Paul?" she said as if the name conjured an enigma, and she glided past her question: "Once he demanded I go out with him, wearing a sheer dress, nothing under it, and beautiful shoes he chose for me, and dazzling earrings. He took me to a famous restaurant where he was greeted like a king. He told me he wanted to remain aroused throughout. Paul. His games."

24

I ran into Paul at the top of the stairs leaving the library and heading to the sundeck.

"Join me, man."

I should not have feared any tension from the intimate night. It was as if it had not happened.

On the sundeck, he went to the bar to fix what would become standard sunning drinks: Cuba libres, ice jiggling in the glasses, frosting them, a sliver of lime perching on each rim. We sat at the bar, under the shade of the canopy, our legs touching, retreating, pressed against each other's, warm, moist, heated by the sun, darkened brown.

Immediately he launched into a tirade, periodically pausing to savor the cold drink, clinking the ice as if in accompaniment to his racing monologue, and quickly moving on, an entangled web of ideas, abruptly taking form. Curt dismissal of writers he didn't admire—including some I had mentioned favorably—followed by breathless homages to those he approved of, and arrogant declamations about how I must expand my influences beyond American writers; declamations and denunciations of psychoanalysts, whom he loathed: "They

destroy all that might be beautiful—blurring with platitudes
the essential considerations of the enigma of evil," that word
"evil" recurring as if floating unattached in his mind, seeking a
definite context, then abandoned, just a word. "Evil." Although
I often disagreed with his conclusions and deductions, I seldom
interjected my contradictions, fascinated by the jumble of ideas,
questions, and suppositions. Increasingly he returned to this: his
interrogation about my "sexual life on the streets." Yet, often, he
interrupted himself to launch into one of his long declamations
of his beliefs—random at times, illogical, at times contradictory,
at times brilliant, at times incomprehensible. Even when he
asked a question, he might tumble over an attempted answer
himself and resume his litany. He seemed to become high on
the flow of his own words, and then he would return to this:

"When you were in what you call a sexual arena—and
I like that, man, a battle, a war—when you were in it, how
many sexual conquests did you achieve? How many, in one
day?" He was speaking fast, as if to gauge it all quickly. "Did
you set a goal, or a record?—or did it just compound like in
your geometric equation that finally coils about itself, or is it
the algebraic one? How many conquests in one day, man, in
the arena?"

"Thirty, in one day."

"Ah."

In my early teens I had worked as a copyboy with the
city newspaper. The number 30 was penciled at the bottom
of a news story to indicate the end. In Griffith Park in Los
Angeles, a huge park in the heart of the city, a park famous as
a "sexual playground" where men gathered for sex along long
trails, miles of roads for driving from one place of encounter
to another, sex everywhere, in pairs or orgiastic groups, in

that park, one day, I set my goal at thirty; but when that was achieved, it was not enough; I needed more victories, more conquests, more "numbers."

"You came thirty times?" he asked me, sipping from the rum drink.

I laughed. "I don't think even you could come thirty times, man. I didn't come at all, just moved from one person to another, being desired, counting."

"You didn't respond? Never reciprocated? You were trade."

I wasn't surprised he knew the word "trade." He was seeking—demanding—indifference, and it had been there in my experiences.

"You never desired the other, right?"

"If I did, I pretended not to, in order to retain my pose of indifference. It was a pose I cultivated."

"Desire depletes—even showing it depletes? Yes! Nothing is more weakening than to desire; yes, I see that, man, I see. All that mattered was your needs, only yours."

As it had been for him, that night with the two women— was he making that connection?

The heat had abated as we sat on the deck drinking chilled wine Paul had opened during dinner. We had left the sundeck and had shifted from the Cuba libres to the white wine he had chosen. Sonya had been unusually restless, perhaps because, earlier, when she had found me and Paul on the sundeck in deep conversation, she had felt left out when Paul went silent.

"I'm going swimming," she had said after dinner.

"This late, Sonya?" I asked, concerned.

"Yes."

"And during those compounded encounters, you felt . . . ?" Paul proceeded.

"Alive while it was all happening—" I started.

"The rush of conquest," he interrupted, "the exhilarating humiliation of the conquered. Desire drains the power to humiliate."

"—and I felt dead when it was over," I finished over his words.

"Alive—dead?" He seemed to be deducing something relevant to himself.

"And sad," I added.

"Sad!" He turned sideways, as if dismissing the compromising word.

"Yes, feeling at times that I had been cruel—"

"Cruel!"

"Yes, cruel in intimate encounters, from one to another, my partners forgotten, encounters in which I was the only one desired, leaving the other feeling . . . erased." Like him, yes; was he listening? The verbalizing of my feelings surprised me. I had not felt that during the sexhunt; those feelings had emerged only now, belated feelings, but I didn't tell Paul that.

"But, man, before you had sex, did you convey your terms?"

"Yes." I knew what was coming, which is what he said:

"Willing victims, man, willing victims," he drew his desired connection.

This was not the time to reject his disturbing deduction; there was more to explore of myself. "Why does all this fascinate you?" I asked him.

He leaned toward me, to add emphasis: "Parallels. Parallels between us, between our lives! Yours and mine. We're two of a kind, man," he said.

Whatever else I might feel for him, I did not admire his life, through which coursed a vein of meanness, of unmitigated selfishness, and cruelty. Had such a vein coursed through my own life? I had to reject it. "I don't think so, Paul, I don't think we're two of a kind."

"Oh, no?" His words, his smile—a startling assumption of knowledgeability about me, his bold stare at me, held along with the goddamned smile—made me turn away.

And then, in a wave of anger, what should have occurred to me much earlier (the answer to the question that I had asked myself over and over about his motivation for inviting me here)—even as I supplied answers that I swept away—was this: He had invited me here, fired up by my narratives of excess— the orgiastic profusion of Mardi Gras amid laughing demonic angels, fleeting intimate connections, indifferent excess—and he, Paul, was fired up too by my accounts of vagrant sexual interludes in downtown Los Angeles in the arena of doomed exiles on the very edge with nothing to lose, rage to exist— asserting from all that the parallels he had drawn (I turned to face him)—and believing that through kindred knowledge, as he saw it, I would set down the facts of his sordid life, con- nected to my own, juxtaposed—"two of a kind"—much of his life already delivered to me in "chapters," to be transcribed and reimagined ("by a young writer, his first book"); and along the way—this frightened me—as he explored his life, and as I set it down in intimate detail, I would discover mine, more vividly recalled than when it had occurred, coldly, indifferently, uncaring, cruel—cruel like a sudden memory among others.

(*In a bar in Hollywood:*

(*The man, in his early thirties, ordinary looking, has been buying me drinks, bourbon and water, which I dislike but which at the time seemed an appropriate drink for my pose.*

(*"Are you hustling?" he asks me, tentatively.*

(Not exactly a hustling bar like the ones downtown, but one that provides such a contact occasionally.

(I've "read" this man. He doesn't want a hustler; but, for me, it's late. I don't want to go downtown. I had no car—I often hitchhiked and, often scored that way.

("No, man." I say what he wants to hear.

("Oh, good," he says. "I don't need to pay for sex, you know?"

("You don't have to." I tell him what he fished for. "I'm just looking for a good time."

("Well . . ."

("You got a place, man?"

("Yes," he answers eagerly, uncertain. "You want . . . ?"

("You have a car?"

("Yes, but we don't need one. I live just a couple of blocks away."

("Let's go."

(His house: a neat, careful house in West Hollywood, which is turning into a "gay city"—many gay people, males and females, and older Jewish couples, families, a "good" neighborhood.

(The inside of his house is as pretty as the outside, and it is fussily decorated.

("I decorated it myself," he says.

("Wow, you're real talented."

("Thank you."

(Later in his bedroom: I lie back, "trade," which is what he wants—no reciprocation.

(It's late. After sex, he lies back. I remain beside him—not close—till I'm sure he's asleep. I get up, not especially quietly, I slip on my Levi's, put my shirt over my shoulders. I go to where he placed his pants neatly over a chair. I pull out his wallet. I open it. Several bills, tens and twenties. I take them out—and then put back a couple of the bills and take the rest.

(He stirs. "You're robbing me," he says.

("Go back to sleep," I say in a harsh voice.

(He lies back, crouching in his bed, afraid—which is what I counted on. He begins to weep quietly.

(I pocket the money—I hear his sobs—I get my boots and socks to put on outside. As I walk out, I hear his weeping edging toward the sobs that follow me out.)

Remembered now with Paul, that memory, like bile in my throat, disgusted me only now, not then.

"Two of a kind." Paul smiled.

In my room, afterward, as I lay unable to sleep, the conclusion I had drawn about Paul's motivation—a brash, arrogant assignment to record his life with parallels in mine—lost its quick conviction as firmly as it had assumed it, moving, like other assumptions, into the field of speculations. Too easy for such a complex man; and all that remained was this:

Why did this man "summon" me here?

And this remained: the memory of the man I had deliberately frightened in Los Angeles, his sobs still pursuing me. A willing victim, Paul would say; but he would be wrong: The man had wanted to thwart what happened with his question to me, and I had cunningly lied.

25

I got up early today, choosing to be alone for at least a portion of the day; so early that the moon, lingering past night, remained, pale in the darkened sky.

I wandered about the island, a section of which in its verdure resembled a jungle. Then, as I stood and listened, I thought I heard a murmur winding into the silence. I realized only then that I had been aware of it before and dismissed it: a muffled rumbling like the sound that precedes the shaking of an earthquake; and that quiet murmur seemed to come from beyond the lake, from the devastated island—I had shifted my position to locate it—and from the tangled shadows; and that silent murmur was floating like a dark cloud toward this island.

The sun was out, the strange impression evaporated, created by the foggy lifting twilight, and—

Stanty!

I was startled to come upon him—asleep, I thought—under a cluster of trees. Muffling my footsteps, I started to walk away. "Are you looking for me, John Rechy?" he said.

"Are you lost?"

"Naw," he said, "just sleeping." In a soft voice like a whisper, he said: "I sleep out here sometimes, you know, when I'm—"

I waited for him to finish. His voice had been wistful, a tone I had heard once before when he had stood on the deck staring out at the lake; he had sighed a vague wish.

"—when it's too hot in the house," he finished in a changed voice, as if only now fully awake and sitting up.

"I'm sorry I interrupted you." I continued to walk away— slowly so that he wouldn't think I was walking away from him. I stopped when I heard him behind me.

He hurried ahead to stand before me, facing me.

"You want to know what happened on that island you keep looking toward?" he said.

"What did happen?" I had reacted impulsively, taking him seriously; it was too late to pull back. "How do you know that?"

"I read about it. Inside a book."

Though strange, it was possible that something terrible had occurred on that island; but that would mean whatever had happened would have occurred a long time ago. *The Origin of Evil*—the book that had disappeared—entered my mind; but, no, that was a collection of essays about spurious theories about evil.

"There was—were—a lot of people on the island when it happened," he said, now an excited storyteller.

I anticipated one of his fantastic tales, but I didn't move away. "And—?"

He shook his head as if at the enormity of what he was about to describe. "What happened was . . . horri"—he paused to choose his word—"horrendous, there was a huge fire, people in flames rushed to the lake, it was too late, everything burned, even the trees—everything, nothing left."

He had trapped me into attention—and had trapped him-self. "What about the man you said you saw at a window?"

"That was on the *other* side of the island, not the one that burned," he said easily.

I started to walk away from him, from his outrageous, quick adjustment of his lie.

He called out after me, shifting subjects, like Paul.

"John Rechy, do you love Sonya?"

"I like her a lot." I was guarded, not knowing where he was going.

"I love her," he said. "Do you like my father?"

"I wouldn't be here if I didn't."

"Yeah," he laughed. "That was a silly question, wasn't it?" Again the wistful sad voice: "I love my father more than anything in the world, and he loves me a lot." He had said that so sadly that I thought of Sonya's words about him, about how sad and confused he was.

He dashed away. "I'm going swimming now!" he called back exuberantly.

I meet Sonya in the library; she's returning a copy of *Wuthering Heights*—"my favorite book," she informs me. "One of mine, too," I say, wanting to assert a closeness.

"Do you suppose Catherine and Heathcliff found each other—ever?" she asks me.

I remember her wistful hope that the guillotined French queen might be saved in another iteration of her story. "Yes," I say, "especially since they agreed—at least Catherine did—that they would prefer being together even if that was in hell." I think she frowned at that; and so I add: "Of course I don't think it had to be hell."

She laughs, an acknowledgement that she understood my soothing interjection. "Thank you, my dear John; you've rescued both the French queen and Catherine, just for me."

I join in her laughter, appreciating her unique test of my loyalty to her sentiments, and glad that I expressed it.

"Let's go rowing, shall we?" she says. "Paul's gone to the village and Stanty's with him. So we'll be alone on the beautiful lake, just you and I."

On the lake: I'm rowing smoothly, facing her. She has "taught" me how to row, as easy as I had anticipated. We're both in our bathing suits, augmenting for me a sense of closeness. I tell her about my unexpectedly mellow interlude with Stanty.

"I'm glad. He wants friends. He never speaks about friends even at school. That's why he keeps asking if one is his friend."

"I felt friendly with him for the first time. He even told me what occurred on the neighboring island."

She looks surprised.

"He said he read about it in a book," I tell her, and realize: No, he said he'd read about it "inside a book"—another of his odd expressions I had noted at the time.

"It's a game he plays, how far he can go and be believed," she says in the tender tone she uses when speaking to him or about him.

"He told me he loves you."

"He's told me that. I love him, too. He's hurt that you won't go rowing with him. It would delight him if you did."

"Would that please you?" I knew the answer.

"Yes, because that would make him happy."

"He also told me he loves Paul more than anyone else in the world."

"I don't know what would happen to him if anything or anyone separated them."

"I don't think anything could," I say.

There followed then, between us, a sense of peacefulness, together, rowing on the lake. At least I felt it and hoped she did too. During the silence that followed, I was aware of the sound of the water lapping at the oars.

She removes the wide hat she often wears. She shakes her head, loosening her hair, an extravagant gesture I cherish, even wait for; hers. She leans back, looking up at the graying sky.

I have rowed absently, allowing the boat to drift. Ahead is the deserted island, the closest I've seen the tangle of twisted, dried branches choking their trunks—yellow fragments of leaves on the parched ground. What might have been flowers are scorched, their petals decayed chips amid rubble. There is no sign of life, none.

I turn the boat away from the dying island. I imagined it devoured by flames, people rushing to escape.

Impulsively, I say: "If I ever write about you, I'll describe you as a woman who, if things were otherwise, I—"

"If you didn't prefer men?" she asks. "Do you, entirely?"

"Yes, and yes," I tell her.

"Then, if otherwise, what?"

"Then, if otherwise, I would describe you as a gloriously beautiful and intelligent woman with whom I would fall in love."

"Please kiss me."

Letting the boat drift, I move over to her, and I kiss her on the lips. I feel desire as my body connects with hers. Our lips remain pressed against each other's, her arms curl about me, mine drew her closer, increasing the intensity, the sense of arousal. I ease away from her bronzed body. I return to the oars.

"I'm sorry," she says. "I understand."

But she can't understand, nor will I tell her that my response to kissing her came from the fact that I was kissing her the way Paul kissed her, the way his body pressed roughly against hers, the way—and that was when I withdrew—the way in his lustful kiss he might draw blood.

As we rowed back, reaching the deck, the heat burst with lightning that punctured blackened clouds, releasing torrents of rain. But it stopped as quickly as it had begun, leaving behind only more heat and a sky overcast with dark clouds and sporadic bursts of thunder. Flashes of lightning in the far distance illuminated the dead island as if it was struggling out of the darkness to reemerge.

26

On a day of white heat, I woke to find a note under my door. It was from Sonya. She and Paul were driving early into the village for a part of the day: "If you wake in time and read this note, please join us." Signed "with love," the note was written in a graceful, flowing script, uniquely hers.

I was glad not to accompany them, not together. Because of the intimacy with Sonya on the rowboat, I felt that I would have to reestablish our close friendship, our unique love, beyond the overtones that occurred on the lake. That would have to be done when we were alone. I had begun to see manifestations of what Sonya had perceived in Paul, a distancing from her. He would be overtly rude to her in often sharp jabs.

("Beauty, have you ever in your life succeeded in anything other than being beautiful?" She remained silent, and I interjected:

("If so, man, she's succeeded superbly.")

What continued was the sudden urgency with which he would reach for her.

I was on my way to the sundeck in my trunks when I encountered Stanty—or rather he came running to intercept me—ready for the lake in his trunks.

"Go rowing with me, John Rechy," he said; "come on! Please!" He grasped my hand, to coax me along with him. "Sonya said you would if I asked you. Aw, come on, please."

"Okay," I said easily.

"Good! Let's go." He was running toward the deck, where the boat waited. I helped him undock, pushing the boat easily into the water, which was serene, deep blue. He was happy, and I felt good.

We jumped into the boat. I grabbed the oars—he had seemed about to claim them. Without protest, he sat down, facing me.

I achieved a slow rhythm rowing. Fanning white foam followed us under the diminishing sun.

"You're rowing good—well," he said. "Sonya said so."

It seemed odd to thank him; so I just nodded, smiling.

Not a breeze, no whisper of a breeze, but being on the water made the day seem cooler as the sun began to set.

"Can you row a little bit faster?" he asked.

"Sure I can." I accelerated my rowing, feeling entirely competent.

"We're going slow," Stanty said, "aren't we?"

"Yeah, I guess," I said. I had been rowing away from the vacated island, the mourning house with its rotting branches. When I had automatically glanced toward it, the dismal convergence of shadows of barren trees was smothering the whole island, pushing it out of sight, unreal as a phantom.

"I bet you could row faster if you wanted—right?"

"I bet I could," I said. I accelerated the rowing. I intended to row not far from Paul's island.

"Let's row faster!" Stanty said.

I grasped the oars firmly as he stood up.

"You're going too slow," he said.

I continued rowing at the same pace, only slightly annoyed at his insistence.

"You're not afraid, are you?" His voice had changed, his voice of command.

"No, I'm not afraid."

He remained standing. "Let me row," he said.

"Not yet," I said. "When we go back."

"Come on," he said. "Let me row."

I didn't feel like upsetting the mood of camaraderie. I let him take the oars, which he grasped quickly, and just as quickly, he turned the boat away from where I had steadily directed it. He was rowing fast, much faster. He plunged the oars deep into the water; frothy water agitated under us.

"Stanty—"

He was rowing forcefully in the direction of the desolate island, leaving Paul's island behind.

I said evenly, not trying to indicate my anger, "You're rowing too fast, and—"

"And I *told* you I wanted to go faster, didn't you hear me?" he demanded, his voice harsh.

"I did hear you, but you didn't hear *me* say we were rowing fast enough, and we're going back now."

He clutched the oars, rowing furiously. Faster, faster, faster toward the dead island.

"What the hell are you doing?" I stood unsteadily in front of him.

To add force to his rowing, he arched his body; the boat was slapping at the water. Despite the confidence I had developed with Sonya and later by myself, it was clear that he was an expert. I realized, startled, that we were battling for the boat. "Give me the oars back." I had to stay in control.

Water from the frenzied rowing spattered on my legs. Over the sound of spraying water, he shouted at me: "You don't like me, do you? You never liked me."

Withheld anger swept over my words. "You're right, I don't like you, I don't like you at all."

"But you like my father, don't you?" he thrust at me.

I couldn't think what to answer. My mind was trying to adjust to—and rejecting—what was happening. About us, water sprayed onto the boat.

"You're always trying to be with him alone, on the deck, I've seen you trying to get close to him."

"You're a fucken liar, you stupid punk!"

"You stay away from him, you hear me?"

Any rebuttal would escalate his accusations, and I didn't want to hear what he might be preparing to say. "We're going back. *Give me the fucken oars now!*"

"Sure," he said, "take them!" He released the oars. Adjusting to the interrupted speed, the boat drifted.

Before I could reach for the oars, he stood.

He removed his trunks.

He stood naked before me. "*Now* do you like me?"

I turned away, but too late. I had seen his naked body in a flash, only seconds, and in those seconds I realized what a beautiful man he would become, like Paul. The next moment, his bare flesh repelled me. "Put your fucken trunks back on!"

"I thought you were a queer," he said.

It was as if he had struck me in my stomach, which wrenched into a wave of nausea. "I am, you goddamn bastard, but not for filthy little punks like you, *Constantine!*"

He closed his eyes, as if to gather his rage. "Don't call me that name, and I'm not a little punk!"

"You are a stupid little punk, Constantine, a dirty, fucken liar. Now put your fucken trunks back on and move away so I can row back."

"Queer! Whore! My father told me everything about you, dirty things, ugly things—everything! Dozens of dirty men you had sex with and you knew it was all filthy. *And cruel!*"

Cruel! A borrowed word, not his. Borrowed from whom? This sinister creature, standing there obscenely—his filthy words roiled within me. Cruel—the uncanny accusation that he knew would wound me.

Dizzy with rage, sweat stinging my eyes, I realized only now—feeling it—that a heated breeze had swept along the darkening lake and the boat was drifting, as if it were on its own leading us somewhere unwanted, somewhere as shadowed and decayed and monstrous as this creature before me, the boat floating toward that stagnant island.

"Your father told you all those things about me?" I asked as he stood with his legs spread, balancing himself expertly on the boat and shifting it slightly from left to right, right to left.

"Yeah!—and more!"

"You're lying, Constantine!"

Nothing I had experienced with Paul allowed me to believe this accusatory monster before me.

"I'm not lying!" And he shifted his legs, swaying the boat, right, left, left, right.

"You lie all the time." Cruel—that incongruous word he had pitched so knowingly into an accusation. Where other than from Paul—or Sonya! No. He had heard it from me! I had said that to Paul—and this demonic creature had listened, lurking, to a word I had spoken in regret, in sadness.

Sheer hatred—that was all I felt now, hatred and rage.

He was rocking the boat faster, left, right, left, right, tilting it right and left farther toward the water each time.

"Stop that, you bastard!"

He rocked it harder, fiercely, faster, harder, faster, jumping from side to side, laughing, the water swirling about the boat, the boat slanting.

"You can't swim, can you?" he taunted. "Can you, *Juan*? That's why you're scared. I'm going to make the boat turn over!" he said, and he was jumping up, down, left, right, the boat swaying, tilting. "And you can't swim, can you? You'll drown!"

Struggling to keep my balance, I lunged at him, to grab him, to stop him.

In one flashing movement he thrust his body against mine—*bare flesh, naked flesh, bodies clasped briefer than a moment, longer than the dying day.*

With all the force of my rage, I thrust him away. He struggled to regain his stance. I pushed him into the water. I threw his trunks after him. I thought I saw his hands grasping. I grabbed the oars, rowing away, faster than I thought I could. I was aware only of the sound of the disturbed water—and the heat, the impossible heat, the goddamned heat.

"I'm hurt, I hit something!" he shouted urgently from somewhere in the watery darkness.

I heard flailing in the water.

"I'm bleeding! Lift me up with an oar, hurry!"

I wouldn't believe him. He was an expert swimmer. And a cunning liar.

"I cut myself on something sharp! My leg—I can't swim."

In our struggle or afterward, had he hit himself, become injured?

I rowed toward where he would be. He was faking! If I extended the oar to him, he would drag me down into the angered water.

"*Island! Isl—!*" The last word he attempted to shout was drowned in silence. More silence, only a fading sound of gurgling water.

Was he tangled in something dangerous, was he really hurt, finally unable to swim? I waited.

I saw a hand—his hand—rise out of the water—I saw it, I see it, I know I saw it, I see it grasping for help—no, reaching for the oar to pull me into the deadly depth. As quickly as it had emerged—I saw it, I know I saw it, I see it—the hand sank back into the water.

Suddenly I was afraid for him. The water was black and ominous as the day expired, leaving only a smirch of blemished light, fading. He had disappeared into the dead darkness. I started to row faster to look around for any trace of him. I stopped.

I rowed back to the island. I would tell the others that Stanty was—

Laughing!

He emerged onto the dock wearing the trunks I had thrown at him.

I made my way out of the boat.

"That was fun, wasn't it, John Rechy? I enjoyed that. Did you?"

27

I wondered feverishly as I made my way to my room that night: what will he claim happened on the lake? If he was capable of what he had done, he would be capable of conjuring something else as monstrous, that I attacked him, that I ignored his cry for help, that I—

Paul and Sonya were back, I heard their voices coming from the deck. Was Stanty there already, venting his poison? I went to my room, shaking with anger, trying to devise a plan to deal with whatever he might say. Whatever he claimed, I would face him, challenge his lies.

It was impossible to sleep, even to rest in bed. How had it come to this? In Paul's letter to me, might I find the trajectory that had led me to the boat on the lake with a strange boy on a strange island; I tried to remember Paul's first words to me, in his letter, to find some answer in the beginning: a retrospective inevitability, a detour not taken? I had read his letter several times to the point that I had almost memorized it: "You have opened the door into a world that few people know exists, and you have revealed it with all its exuberance and its hellishness, which you describe in one place as dominated by—I admire this very much—demonic clowning angels."

Sitting under the exposed swirls of liquid colors in the painting over the desk—the towel had fallen—I typed:

I wandered about the island, a section of which in its verdure resembled a jungle. Then, the sense of isolation that the island created by its very nature was intensified, a silence wound into the heat of days, a sense of invited isolation, and I remembered, "Island! Island!"—a mantra between him and Stanty, a sense of owning and ruling over their own world, my role still undefined. The heat, the silence, the oppressive verdure, the placid lake that seemed at times to contain buried tensions—yes, and the vacated island entangled in shadows—it was all that which made me afraid.

I woke up in a bed of sweat. I was not ready, not prepared yet, to face anyone. I would stay in my room, keep the door closed. Restless, I got up and looked out the window when I heard voices. I saw Sonya walking with Stanty along the edge of the lake, her morning stroll, usually alone. What was he telling her? Even from this distance, she seemed serious, attentive.

I tried again to read. The words floated in my mind, incomprehensible. I heard a soft knock on the door. Sonya? I remained quiet, pretending to be asleep, and soon I did fall asleep again, black, oppressive sleep.

At dinner, Sonya was the first to ask where I had been all day; "I worried that you might be sick," she said. Paul greeted me as usual, a smile, a few muffled words, "man." Stanty sat at his usual place—again eating scoops of jam.

I looked away from him. The explosive silence melded with the heat and the ineffective whirring of the new electric fan.

On the deck . . .

Sonya looked perturbed, perhaps only because I had not answered her knocking, if it had been she who knocked. I hadn't spoken much since I had joined them. Now Paul and Sonya were talking, something about the village; and I responded automatically, faking attention. Paul was lounging in his deck chair—waiting? Sonya sat next to him, smoking at intervals from his cigarette. I tried to discern some signal of what they, either of them, might know. No clue in the heated silence.

Constantine—I wanted to think of him only as that, the name he detested—leaned against the railing facing the deepening hue. The sight of him, the memory of his body pressed against mine for seconds, revolted me to the point that I could not even glance at him. Was it possible that he had revealed nothing yet?—all dormant within unbudging silence.

Which was about to explode.

Stanty had turned to face us all, I knew from the sudden attention of the others.

He said: "Look! It's the blue hour. We sure—surely—have ignored it a lot, haven't we?—the time when everything is revealed. Isn't that so, John Rechy?"

I had only seconds to prepare for what was coming. He had waited for the blue hour, to use as his own against me.

I waited; alerted silence waits.

Stanty said to Paul, "I wanted to teach John Rechy how to row, but Sonya taught him already, and real good—well."

"Did you enjoy rowing with Stanty, man?" Paul asked me.

"Of course he did," Sonya said.

If I were to write about what followed after the violence on the lake, I would change it because what did happen, what is happening now, is too challenging for fiction.

Nothing happened.

The next morning, in the library, Stanty greeted me as usual.

"Good morning, John Rechy."

Those ordinary words, spoken by him, assumed a malignancy that pitched me back into the mixture of feelings he had aroused, all coalescing into hatred. I didn't move. Could I become like the others on the island—like him, ignore the horrendous event, everything forgotten, everything resuming as before, all unmentioned, left abandoned, an unspoken code on this island?

I walked out without acknowledging him. I returned to my room, and wrote:

> Constantine—I wanted to think of him only as that, the name he detested—leaned against the railing facing the deepening hue. Was it possible that he had revealed nothing yet?—all dormant within an explosive silence.
>
> Then:
>
> He turned to face us all.
>
> I had only seconds to prepare for what was coming. He had waited for the blue hour, to use as his own against me.

If I were to write about what happened on the lake and what followed, I would change it all, because what did happen is too challenging for fiction.

Angrily, furious, I wrote this:

I had only seconds to prepare for what was coming. He had waited for the blue hour, to use as his own against me.

He said, "We were rowing, John Rechy and me—I— and all at once he—"

I interrupted him, facing him. "What he's about to tell you is a goddamned lie, like so many others he tells and you pretend to believe him. The dirty little bastard tried to drown me—"

Even in the dark, I saw Paul's face contort in anger as he stood up to face—

I yanked the piece of paper out of the typewriter and I ripped it into pieces.

Paul and I sat alone on the deck drinking wine. Beyond, nebulous forms twisted on the lake, misty silhouettes like ghosts ushering in the night. It was after dinner. Sonya, just joining us, had cooked something—I don't remember what. I had not seen Stanty since our latest intersection in the library. I considered that he might be avoiding me, and I hoped that he was.

Paul had resumed his accusations of Elizabeth, so overtly, so relentlessly accusatory and ridiculing that I wondered what had occurred now to incite his renewed assault, at times blurted out, phrases, unfinished sentences, a composite judgement against the first woman he had married, words tumbling over words as he drank his favorite wine—which he held out to Sonya, his glass, to sip from.

"Elizabeth's life was a series of 'consultations,' devoted to unhappiness, hers and everyone else's, a lover of psy-cho-anal-y-sis"—always chopping the word to express his contempt—"an expert analysand, trekking from fraud to fraud, until she found the superfraud, the idiotic Dr. Spitzer, who introduced her to his"—adopting an odd accent I couldn't identify—"Radical Theory of a Psycho-Balanced Universe Through 'Reverse Interplay,' as propounded in his self-published book, and that would 'purge away' all that chafed in her life since she was not responsible for anything, nothing!" He paused breathless in his asseveration. "Or something like that," he added, and rushed on gleefully:

"She grew fond of all the dredged-up rot, bragged about it, came to love it—listen to this, man—and all of that was what she presented to me as her credentials, like a gift, to show that she was worthy of me, and"—he laughed, terrible laughter, and sipped the rest of the wine in his glass, handing it over to Sonya for her to fill again and she did, and filled mine—"and—and—and—grasp this, man—with all her malignancy, she did prove she was worthy of me. And so I married her."

His lashing of Elizabeth extended into the following afternoon when we—he and I and Sonya—were on the sundeck, sitting on stools at the bar under the shadow of the tree lurking outside and over the vine-draped wall enclosing the deck.

"We were the perfect couple, everyone said so; Paul and Elizabeth, what a lovely rotten couple, made for each other. Have I told you about the emotional slaughter we conspired to bring about, like happy devastating children?"

"You have told us that," Sonya said with a forced smile. Rising from her stool—she was wearing a red bathing suit that seemed to embrace her—she touched her lips, lightly, a motion that suggested she had heard enough and would contribute nothing. With a slight nod toward Paul, another toward me, she left.

"Did I tell you, man, that I matched Elizabeth, then surpassed her—?"

"At dangerous games?"

"Yes; and I matched her in meanness—your word, no, man?"

"Yes, man—my word—and you did tell me."

"That she was selfish and greedy—"

"Like you, yes."

"—a mad puppet manipulated by her equally insane parents?"—ignoring my words, or not having heard them, and jiggling the ice in his second Cuba libre (I had only one)—he went on to ravage her family: "She was faithful to a family tradition: Her father, who became an ambassador to somewhere, specialized in creating crises so he could get credit for solving them; her mother took up painting—miniatures, of course, all she could grasp, tiny ugly things, like their brains. Two monsters churned in grinding copulation to produce another monster whom they named Elizabeth."

I said, angered by his tirade: "Since you saw what made her a monster, is she still a monster?" I wanted to yank him away from his self-appreciated "meanness," a word he annoyingly kept attributing to me.

"Of course she still is, man—what the hell? Surely you understand all this," he said, "since you witnessed the reign of clowning angels fighting for beads on a filthy street—and you saw that so fucken clearly." His unexpected laughter was so raucous that he—untypically—spewed out what he had been drinking, a stream of liquor that drizzled on my oiled body and slid off. The sharp gray shadow slicing the sunlight had done little to reduce the heat, but at that moment a breeze glided over us and alerted me that I was sitting close enough to feel the heat radiating off Paul's body. Remembering Stanty's accusations, I swung my bar stool away, and then the same anger, increasing with remembered bile, pulled me back, closer.

"During all those terrible, long years, man, when did you finally decide to fucken leave her?" I asked him, feeling angrier now at him.

He shook his head. "Man? What? Oh, of course, when I met Corina and her filthy millions, that's when I left Elizabeth. It was time."

The audacious declaration, the bragging, the self-affection, the vaunted coldness, the scheming, and, yes, the meanness, the absurdity—I blurted out the laughter I had been withholding at his rant. He joined me easily as if he, too, had considered it all amusing, and then he was quiet, listening.

I was aware of the sound of the motorboat in the distance, approaching. It would be the gray couple, leaving or returning, but at an unusual time. The sound stopped.

Sonya entered the sundeck. She stood for a few moments, as if to gain our full attention.

"Elizabeth is here," she said.

28

At the top of the slope, before the front entrance to the house, stood Elizabeth.

This was the monster Paul had described: an elegant woman, tall, slender, wearing slacks and a loose thin blouse, expensive clothes—I will determine that later, since now Sonya and I are approaching her from a distance—which she displayed perfectly. She might have been beautiful—I saw this as we came closer to her—had she not underplayed that aspect of herself. Subtle makeup—this became apparent when we reached her—seemed faintly drawn to emphasize high cheekbones, a face framed by dark hair. She is looking about the landscape, her head tilted quizzically, like a queen surveying new territory. Even the long shadow she casts before her asserts command, a woman sure of her imposing appearance, and entirely composed.

She is smiling.

This, then, was the reason for Paul's reiteration of charges against her: He had known she was coming; he had alerted the gray ghosts, the gray couple; and he had, with all the vitriol he had enunciated against her, prepared the atmosphere for her arrival, spreading to all of us his welcome.

Earlier on the sundeck, Paul had stood up when Sonya made her announcement; he wiped himself with a fresh towel, and without a word he walked away. Sonya had remained with me on the deck—I had stood up to join her.

"She did come," she said quietly, as if determined to be at ease. "Do you suppose the other wife will come?"

I shrugged, wondering the same.

Stanty's voice called out, urgent, loud, untypical: "Father, Elizabeth is here." His voice, remembered from the deadly night, made me turn away from its direction.

Smiling—preparing a smile—Sonya put on her hat. Steadily she lit a cigarette—unusual for her—from the pack abandoned by Paul. She inhaled, puffed out the smoke in one single plume, stubbed out the cigarette on her hand, like Paul—and she flipped it angrily away.

I readied myself to offer what I could to assuage her, whatever would occur. I put my arm about her waist. She touched my hand and smiled. "She's going to love you, like I do."

"I'm not concerned about her," I said as we left the sundeck, "and I love you, too." Declarations not of love but of allegiance.

Stanty was standing a distance away from the woman at the entrance to the house. The male of the gray couple was carrying a small suitcase; the female followed him into the house.

Paul is walking toward Elizabeth.

All assumed a kind of choreography about her.

I stand back to allow Sonya to go ahead.

The two women face each other—Sonya, boldly beautiful; and Elizabeth, in comparison, almost severe in her commanding presentation—both Paul's women, Elizabeth perhaps now the woman she had become, not the one she had been.

"Sonya, I suppose," Elizabeth greeted her.

"Elizabeth, I suppose." Sonya's tone was cool. The two women mimed a kiss, a touch, cheek to cheek, again on the other side, on Sonya's part a formality, demanded.

Stanty walked up, close to Sonya.

Staring at the tall somber iron statues, which had been returned to the lawn, Elizabeth said to Paul, who had advanced to meet her with a light kiss, returned cursorily: "You acquired those, too; you always wanted them."

"Yes," he answered easily, "and I had them brought out to greet you."

"A steely greeting," she smiled. "Those two who brought me here in the boat—the woman in the village said they—"

Paul interrupted her. "I assume you've—"

She rejected his interruption: "—where did you find them?"

Stanty stood in his rigid position, like a sentinel, as if that would shelter him from whatever might unfold.

Paul, ignoring the pending question, resumed: "I assume you've been granted a brief sabbatical from Dr.—what is his name? You told me. Or is he a new one?"

She raised her hand before her, dismissing the question. "Paul, really," she said.

I held back, not wanting to intrude on whatever further conversation they might reserve for each other.

By the time I did join them, they all stood in the large living room, like chess pieces anticipating a strategic move.

"This is John Rechy, the writer I wrote to you about," Paul said to Elizabeth as he went about filling everyone's glass—but not Stanty's, not even the usual few drops—with the expensive wine that he preferred. He raised his glass in a vague salute.

Elizabeth—about Paul's age, I determined—held out her hand to me, and I took it. I continued to marvel at the woman standing before me, not the mad jagged creature Paul had described.

She had just read what Paul had sent her by me, she told me. "I admire the intimacy of your work," she said. Her cultured tone was natural, not strained, easy, inherited from her famous intellectual father and mother.

"Thank you." I glanced at Paul, hoping to convey my astonishment at this unexpected presence.

"Paul sent me a copy of a story you wrote—'The Fabulous—'"

"'—Wedding of Miss Destiny,'" I finished for her, to obviate her stumbling over my title.

She said: "When he told me he had invited you here, I read it, wondering what he had responded to so strongly, perhaps intimately."

Just as I still wondered.

She continued, "I can see how Paul would be smitten by your writing. He is an expert pursuer of—perhaps I should call him a hound in pursuit of talent. I've often supposed he believes he can absorb it. Especially," she added, "from attractive talent."

"You make me sound like a vampire," Paul laughed.

"You may be," she said, smiling back. "But you're also a sensational thief. Have you discovered that to be true, Sonya?"

"I have nothing to be stolen," she said.

"You're modest," Elizabeth said. "Beauty is most easily exploited, with cunning." She accused Paul: "Your description of her didn't do her justice. She is even more beautiful than I expected. Will Corina be here?"

"Will she, Father?" Stanty asked.

"Do you want her to come?" Elizabeth asked him. Nothing in her tone indicated that she had been disturbed by Stanty's query, or his tentative presence. He was untypically quiet, seeming confused, remaining close to Sonya.

Paul shrugged. "I believe Corina's in Salzburg—I'm not sure. She never announces her visits; she comes when she wants."

"It's still her island?" Elizabeth said.

"Father!" Stanty reacted in anger. "It's *our* island!"

"Of course it is," Paul assured him. "Remember when we first came here?"

"Yes, yes!" Stanty said eagerly. "Island! Isl—"

"Dear Paul," Elizabeth interrupted him. "Who are you trying to convince, and, more important, why? Have you finally acquired a sense of . . . oh, no, no, please not. Don't lose your shamelessness, it's a major part of your charm. You extorted the island from Corina, just as you did the statues—and what else? The paintings, and—a major feat, considering the wrath of her father. I've wondered how you made her your powerful ally throughout your fight for what I believe you call alimony." She continued as Paul remained silent, "I believe the father wanted you removed from their lives entirely, to make you invisible. He approved anything that would send you away."

To whom was this information being delivered, information that both of them knew? It had to be part of her purpose in being here, to inform. Whatever that purpose was, nothing about her indicated apprehension about her intent.

"Corina gave everything to me, all of it. She encouraged her father to agree," Paul said calmly.

"She gave you everything." Elizabeth smiled, shaking her head. "Including, of course, Stanty."

I saw Sonya wince; she drew Stanty closer to her, as if to protect him from the harsh words.

"The island is mine and my father's," Stanty said.

"Of course it is," Elizabeth said. Then to Paul: "She gave you everything you have, you charming—" She turned to face me and held up her glass as in a belated toast. "What is the word? Hustler?"

Directed at Paul, or at me? At both of us?

"Aren't we all?" I said.

"Charming?" Elizabeth turned to me.

"No, hustlers."

Elizabeth laughed easily. "Except for Stanty," she added. "He's still waiting to become—what will you become?"

"I—" Stanty looked at Sonya, he looked at Paul, as if for urgent help. "Father?" he transferred the question to him.

"A reflection of your father," Elizabeth answered her own question. "That is what you will become." She addressed Stanty in the eerily unchanged tone of easy banter.

Paul said to Stanty: "Nobody will determine who you will be." The first note of anger, quickly suppressed.

"Except you, Father?"

Did he realize he had echoed Elizabeth? He looked at Sonya, he looked at Paul, as if he needed help. I had thought it impossible that I would ever feel sorry for him; the memory of what had occurred on the lake with him was implanted in my mind. For the first time he seemed lost. I rejected any feeling of compassion.

Sonya held on to Stanty's hand, as if to claim him. What was she inferring about all this? How much did she know? Elizabeth was not here for a visit; she had arrived with scant luggage. The placid undercurrent that I had often detected was being disturbed, still barely perceptibly.

Paul had not responded to Elizabeth's taunting words, flung at him in soft tones—and with cool smiles—as if in guaranteed agreement between them, a keen knowledge of each other's tolerance for private insults. Yet Paul's acquiescence in the polite, deadly exchange might be in anticipation of breaking all existing boundaries between them.

Paul joined Sonya, a slide toward her, away from Elizabeth. I was relieved. That might signal a lowering of the impatience he had begun to show her. He placed his arm about her waist: alliances forming, reinforced? Rigidly silent, Stanty seemed to be waiting.

All of us gathered here are waiting.

29

We went to our rooms to change for dinner from our daily casual fashion—Elizabeth's manner conveyed an expectation of at least a modicum of formality.

When we regrouped we were still informally dressed, but less so, Sonya in a gossamer violet dress that, as she moved, revealed slashes of golden flesh. As if, even in this, we were involved in competition—which annoyed me—both Paul and I wore khakis and white shirts (I rolled the sleeves up). Only Stanty had remained stubbornly as he had been.

Sonya arranged the table, casually as always, and lit the candles. Paul set the prepared dinner—thin-sliced filet mignon, a leafy salad, cheese, fruit, and, of course, excellent wine.

During dinner, there was none of the usual light talk among people who have not seen each other for some time. The sense of waiting stretched within the darkened glow of the candles, flickering occasionally when swept by the swirling of the electric fan.

Dinner was over. There was the usual lull in conversation as we waited for a hint of what would come next, drinking the wine, spearing pieces of fruit, and choosing cheese.

Stanty stood straight up in his chair, his military style of command recovered.

"Elizabeth, why are you here?" he asked.

"I love this wine, Paul," Elizabeth said, sipping it slowly.

"I got it in anticipation of your visit, Elizabeth."

"It's much like the Sancerre we drank one night in Constantinople," she said. Then: "Stanty, what did you ask me?"

I had seen Stanty wince at the mention of Constantinople. With a smile, Paul fixed his gaze on him, granting permission. His stance regained, Stanty repeated, "I asked you, Elizabeth: Why? Are? You? Here?"

"To see what kind of life you've been living on this isolated island," she said.

In silence, disoriented by her ambiguous declaration, everyone stared at her as if, even without further clarification or direction from her, no more words were needed.

She sipped more wine. Another pause. She sipped again, delighting in its taste, commenting on it. She was withholding whatever she was about to say, keeping it in abeyance, feeding the attention she was demanding while asserting her composure. Taking another sip, holding the glass out, all in smooth motions. She said: "Please, Paul, a toast. We haven't had one, a toast to this memorable evening."

Equally assured—two generals who have measured each other's strengths and weaknesses and are preparing to kill—Paul raised his glass: "To this fucken memorable evening, whatever it is."

Out of context, or expectation, the bold word, pronounced in mockery of Elizabeth's suggestion, did not jar her; she showed not even the slightest frown of displeasure: "Why is it, Paul, that you force yourself to become vulgar; usually that's only in reference to sex. Why?"

"Sex?" he said. "Elizabeth, sex is vulgar, it has to have its own language. Without vulgarity—crassness, yes—sex is only tedious; you should know that, the tedium of exhausted desire. Some resort to dangerous games."

"Like you, Paul; just like you."

"Like us." he corrected her. "Just like us."

"Yes," she agreed. "We played together."

A time when, Paul had claimed, she had colluded in being cut with a knife, allowing blood to trickle onto her breasts, to be licked off by him—that recalled vision too was in total conflict with the woman before us.

She was looking at me, addressing me: "Has he enlisted you in one of his games? Perhaps not played yet? He plots them carefully, you do know?" It was clear she expected no answer as she held her glass out to be refilled by Paul, who did so.

What game, for me? I wouldn't be a part of Paul's maneuvers; I was never less than his equal, even more. I dismissed my brief displeasure—Elizabeth was moving only to separate possible allegiances with Paul.

She rose from the table and walked over to Stanty and touched his shoulder. He shook his head, rejecting her gesture.

"Stop that, I'm too old for that," he protested angrily.

"But you're not," she said. To Paul: "Have you given any thought to his future? I don't mean the scheming manipulation you've exposed him to; I mean a future without you." It was as if words of anger, of accusation, had been borrowed to be spoken in a light drama, out of place. There would be more, I felt sure, much more about Stanty, more that was painful, cruel, beyond strange. That was why she was here.

"What will happen to him?" Paul responded easily. "At the end of summer he'll go back to school, then he'll return to me, always."

What will happen to Stanty? After a series of expensive schools, what? I wondered. On this island, the two together, father and son, masters of their world, invaded only by invitation. Father and son.

"I stopped at the realtor's office yesterday in the village," Elizabeth said, moving to the open glass doors as if to sample the night. "I asked about the vacant island."

Stanty tilted his head, to listen.

"You intend to buy it?" Paul said sarcastically.

"No one will," Elizabeth said flatly, turning to face us. "In the village there's renewed talk about what happened there."

"You listened to those people?" Paul asked in mock indignation, or to stop her from going on.

"I know their malice," Elizabeth said. "They never liked us; we're not their sort, too rich, too educated—and strange, they said"—she smiled—"remember, Paul?"

"You never cared," Paul reminded her.

"I still don't," Elizabeth said. "But, now, there's more. The rumors involve Stanty, and seriously."

Stanty stood up abruptly. "What rumors?"

Elizabeth proceeded slowly, softly, unaroused. "That you claim you know everything about that island, that you insist there's someone there now, and that you've seen him. There are wild suppositions, about a fire, about a possible drowning—and more, much more; you bragged about that in the village when Paul went to talk to the lawyer and left you in the restaurant."

Sonya said, "That isn't so, I was with both of them all that time."

We were all standing now; the arena was changing.

"No, my lovely, you went with Paul." Elizabeth tossed the words at her. "Stanty went to the restaurant."

"I know that woman who talked about me," Stanty said, and then to Paul: "Father, she's that ugly waitress. She asked all kinds of dirty questions about what goes on on our island, and I said stuff to shut her up. She tried to kiss me, and I pushed her away—she stank awful—"

A drowning. My memory of the day on the rowboat—I turned away from Stanty in a rush of rage. A drowning—and more, much more.

"Why are you here, Elizabeth? We've been asking," Paul said, with an edge of impatience, a signal of anger.

Elizabeth said: "I'm here to take my son away from you."

Paul laughed, mirthless laughter.

Stanty turned swiftly to face Elizabeth: "I'm not going anywhere with you. You're not my mother."

"I am your mother." Elizabeth moved closer to him; he jerked away. Elizabeth faced Paul: "With reliable and expensive advice, I have arrived at the decision that it is essential to tell Stanty the tawdry story before I take him away from you."

"Father!" Stanty said in panic, swinging about to face Elizabeth. "You aren't my mother. . . . Father!"

"I *am* your mother," Elizabeth continued. "Paul tried to convince you that I'm not, I let him, I encouraged it, I didn't want you, I detested you because you were his."

I wondered: When will this woman's iron composure crack? Can she sustain this icy calm throughout these damning declarations?

Smoothing her hair back carefully, she resumed addressing Stanty, who had moved close to Sonya, who hugged him. "I tried to keep you from being born. But you—and Paul—were determined. You clawed your way out of me, pulling yourself out with my blood." She paused to assert her violent litany, the horror in benign words. She will stop; she can't go on.

She went on, as if fascinated by the words she was flinging into the hot silence. "I wished you had drowned in the blood you drained from me."

And then: another lethal pause, as if time must stop to allow more fatal words, which she aimed at Stanty. "Corina didn't want you, either, but she took you because Paul convinced her that it would ensure her connection with him, make it permanent, bind them to each other," she said in a sarcastic tone. "Of course he was lying. His goal was to ensure his fortune—and to keep you to himself, to own you. Only his—no despised women allowed. I'm sorry, my lovely"—she addressed Sonya—"but you do know he detests women, *all* women."

Sonya flinched, as if physically wounded. Quickly recovering, she aimed her words at Paul: "How can you allow this woman to continue? Those dreadful lies." She held Stanty closer to her.

"Because," Paul said, "what she's saying is true."

"Father—" Stanty began, again beseeching, again frantic.

Of all the terrible things I had learned about on this island, what I was hearing was the most frightening. I longed to believe that this, like all the other damning scenes, would be gone by morning, forgotten. But as I look at the players in this drama, I know that this time it will not happen.

Elizabeth delivered her case like an expert prosecutor, convinced of her victory. "It may be difficult to believe," she addressed us all, "that Paul is a man of strict morality, his own; he is capable, as few people are, of seeing himself, judging himself, the way he sees and judges others. You have surely heard him rant about the vileness of mankind"—all delivered with sarcasm—"the evil he sees everywhere, the greed, anger, yes, all that. But whenever he lists the horrors he sees in the world, he adds— Paul, please, your words; I couldn't do justice to your refined audacity."

Paul answered: "Rot and decay to which—"

"Yes. That's it," Elizabeth interjected with a tinge of excitement, "everyone, listen: to which—"

Paul finished: "—to which I have added more than my share."

"How moral, how perfectly moral, and how proud he is: to decry the forces that you join, to judge them and confess your allegiance to them. Paul, how brave!"

As if the anger had achieved a physical force, bombarding them, Sonya's arms about Stanty seemed to want to shelter him.

"You love her?" Elizabeth asked Stanty. "Yes, I see that, and she will be allowed to love you, until Paul is through with her—is he yet?—and then you will hate her, too. Like Paul. No women will be allowed." She smiled, a slash of pale color across the perfect whiteness of her face. "All that is over. I'm here to save Stanty from all that."

Stanty fired at her: "You go away, leave me alone, leave my father alone, go away, Elizabeth, I hate you as much as you hate me, go away, leave me alone. *Father!*"—pleading for help. "Island!" he shouted in panic. "Island!"

"He won't go with you, ever," Paul said.

"I will fight you, Paul," Elizabeth threatened.

"You won't."

Elizabeth sighed—a long sigh—and then she said: "It would be scandalous to reveal everything publicly, but if necessary, so be it. Of course, you do know that if that occurred, Corina's powerful father"—she paused, as if considering deeply—"or even mine, would kill you. Both despise you."

"Why do you want Stanty now, after all those years, after all that hatred even before he was born?" Sonya's voice, the determined firmness with which she was questioning Elizabeth, surprised me.

Elizabeth separated herself from everyone. She faced us all. "Because," she said—

She will break now, the composure will crash—

"—I want finally to be . . . a good mother. I want my son to be with me."

Time stopped; all sound had stopped. Through the open glass doors, fierce, hot darkness invaded in slapping waves.

Then:

"I want," Elizabeth said, "to undo the horror of it all, to undo—"

And then:

"To undo?" Paul threw his head back and laughed, a loud, harsh laugh. Slowly at first, then rapidly, he brought the palm of one hand against the other, then again, fast, again, faster, louder—applauding and laughing at the same time. "What a fucken performance, Elizabeth! Goddamn if you didn't almost—I say, almost—have me!"

"I've done what I had to do." It was an announcement that she had finished her delivery, precise, clear, steely.

"You've done what your lunatic psychiatrist told you to do, his stupid assignment," Paul said, "stupidly to try to undo rancid years that we—yes, you and I—formed together. And you want to undo your guilt with this fucken reckless act? What a fucken performance!" He shook his head as if genuinely disappointed in her.

"Yes, of course, to everything, yes, yes, yes—and it's all done," Elizabeth said, and her voice had not changed. "I've undone it all, yes, and I'm leaving now," she said. "I told the two zombies you employ to wait for me, to take me to the shore, to my car."

Had this performance truly happened? Over now, it seemed impossible. But there was Paul, trying now to control his laughter, and there was Sonya with tears dampening her face, and there was Stanty looking pale, angry. On this island of extremes—an island that seemed to have the power of manipulation, as if it had created and allowed all that had occurred, and more that surely might occur—on this island, Elizabeth's contrivance had assumed its place, one more heinous event to add to the others.

Elizabeth walked over to Sonya.

I thought: She's preparing her exit, a part of her staged, redemptive scene, to restore—I almost laughed aloud—balance to the "universe."

"You're the most beautiful of Paul's women," she said to Sonya. "When Paul is through with you—he may already be—is he, my lovely, is he?"

Sonya seemed to freeze, as if she had stopped breathing.

I thought: Is Elizabeth right?—is that already happening?—what Sonya had suspected, and now Elizabeth had added her knowledge of his detestation of women; had Sonya ever heard that before? Had Paul gone that far? From her sudden look of bewildered anger at Paul, I knew Sonya was hearing those words of Paul's total hatred for the first time—Elizabeth had struck expertly.

"—when that happens," Elizabeth continued addressing Sonya, "perhaps you will look me up." Holding her tightly as Sonya attempted to resist, Elizabeth kissed her on the lips, a long hungry kiss.

Sonya twisted forcefully away, rubbing the kiss off with her hand, then holding her palm open, staring down at it as if in shock, then wiping her hand furiously against her body.

As we heard the roar of the motorboat outside, Elizabeth walked to the door. She stood with her back to us. Then she turned to face us—

—and I saw this:

Her facade remained composed, she remained composed; but—

I saw this:

Her hands clenched into tight, angry fists that she held against her body as if to control them; and she said:

"I am not to blame. I have no guilt. I have reversed it all."

30

We've been living in episodes, though with players in common, each episode an entity in itself; and each episode disappears, undiscussed, pushed into silent limbo. Reminding myself of that is my way of sustaining the hope that the enormity of Elizabeth's incursion, as harrowing as it was, will, in the same inexplicable way as other such events, be banished as if it never happened, leaving behind not even the faintest scent of its poison. (Is that possible for me? Can I ever forget the whirling water waiting to suck me in that fateful night?)

I get out of bed, realizing that I was so distracted last night that I can't remember what I had intended to read. A book by Henry James lies on the floor beside the bed; it's his story of exact ambiguity. The painting is covered with a towel that I placed over it last night. I'll leave it covered, to shove away its threat.

WHWACK!!! WHWACK!!!

I recognize sounds of firing. Stanty practicing with Paul again. Or is he alone, learning? Has Sonya agreed to teach him?

I go to the drawer where I left the sheets I had been typing. These entries are an obvious narrative account of the events on this island from the beginning, Paul's invitation. No, I will never write about this island. Its mysteries baffle me. How can I record what I don't understand?

I head for the sundeck. Despite my conviction that nothing of last night's chaos will be addressed, I feel trepidation when I see Stanty heading toward the boathouse. When he sees me, he stops, as I do—I'm sure for the same reason: we do not want to encounter each other, and have not done so since that turbulent time on the lake. My detestation of him is almost threatened by the unwelcome recollection of him clinging to Sonya in panic as Elizabeth hurled her calm revelations of hatred toward him, like soft curses. That image is not enough to temper my rage.

I don't move, conflicted about what to do as he continues toward me. "Good morning, John Rechy," he says, and I know that he is leaving the intended bloodying of last night dormant, like the attempted drowning on the lake.

I cannot answer him, cannot acknowledge him. I continue to the sundeck. There is no way that I saw what I think I saw in that flashing instant of encountering him. I could not have seen that his eyes were red, as if he'd been crying. Stanty crying? Totally my imagination, which I imposed on him. Besides, he had been wearing sunglasses when we crossed paths.

Paul and Sonya are lying on mats; but they have placed them under the shade of the tree whose overhanging shade falls daily onto the sundeck and then lengthens and shortens as the day passes and sunlight shifts.

With the usual words of greeting and cursory inquiry—and I'm still being attentive to even a nuance of last night's emotional turbulence, and of any new knowledge of the events on the lake—I join the two at the edge of the shade, which makes our bodies appear even darker, gleaming with oil, a sensual sight that softens my anxiety.

As I lie on my pad, I notice that the shade has darkened earlier than I remember; it's the first signal of summer's waning. That thought saddens me, the ending of summer, and that arouses in me a sense of another ending, a powerful one, final, along with a sense of urgency, of incompleteness. This mixed feeling is so assertive that I am sure, for a disoriented moment during which the shade we're lying on stretches even more, that the others are feeling it, too, and as powerfully. What the urgent incompleteness is, I don't know. Through those bewildering thoughts courses a sense of sorrow.

"Man?"

I hadn't noticed, during those odd seconds, that Paul had gotten up and is extending to me a tall Cuba libre.

"We got ahead of you," Sonya says, sitting up exhibiting her own glass. She's smiling, her most brilliant, loving smile. The smile is so tempting that I reach out to touch her lips. I stop just short of accomplishing that—and she laughs. I laugh with her, at nothing, really. Elizabeth's assault, her prophecy of Paul's abandoning her, has had no discernible effect.

"I'll try to catch up," I say to Paul, only because he seems to be waiting for some kind of agreement. He seems uncommonly exuberant.

He is lying next to Sonya in the sheltering shade, and we all three join in laughter at an unknown situation. With a start,

I notice this: The sunlight, still harsh, is stretching afternoon shadows—longer, longer, longer—toward the white borders of the sundeck. The angle of the shadows has shifted, too, bringing this day to an earlier close.

Paul is smoking more than usual, now and then handing his cigarette over to Sonya for a brief puff. He seems especially edgy—even nervous—no, anxious—no, eager. All of that affirms my supposition that the feeling I have of an ending without completeness, asserted by the conspiracy of shadows preparing for summer's end—hints, slight changes, and no diminishing of the heat—is shared by him.

He has just returned from the village. "I bought some new records, some especially for each of you," he says. He speaks the rest like a prepared announcement, again suggesting to me his unfocused urgency: "We can listen to them tonight, what do you say, beauty?"

"If you want, yes," Sonya says.

"Man?" he asks me.

"Yeah, great ... man," I wonder what record or records he may have selected based on his assumption about my taste, another aspect of his character: a firm belief in his assumptions. He seems eager for approval of his planned concert.

We go inside the house when the sun has declined, etching dark shadows on the sundeck.

The gray couple has prepared an appropriately cold dinner. It's late evening, and the two have disappeared. During the glimpses I have caught of them, I have never seen them other than with their eyes cast down. They exist like wakened somnambulists.

Paul has chosen an "extra-special wine" for dinner, although we have not abandoned our unfinished Cuba libres.

"A toast to tonight's concert," he says as he opens the wine.

We retreat with our drinks to the deck. The night is suffused with a strange light, a mixture of the light of the moon, brighter than I have seen it, as it disentangles itself out of fragments of flimsy clouds. I wonder what Stanty might make of this moody, commanding illumination. But he's not here. Will I ever again experience a "blue hour" like the one that has become a part of this island?

"Paul insisted Stanty retire early tonight; he looked tired," Sonya informs me about Stanty's absence. "He loves to sleep outside."

I imagine him outside—as I found him that one day; imagine him searching for the darkest shadows to sleep under.

Paul is pouring more wine—"the very best!"—into our glasses. The glass in his hand tilts and falls, umber liquid spilling onto the floor; pieces of sharp-edged glass assumed a distorted shape. Staring down at the watery smirch, a liquid puzzle, Paul frowns and abruptly reminds us of his plan. We will all go down to the lower depth of the house, a floor that includes, but separately, the library and the smaller room with the large locked box with the gun. That thought—irrelevant, I know—strikes me with the impact of an actual shot.

Sonya is bending to gather the glassy jetsam off the floor, and for no reason laughs, infectious laughter that Paul joins in, and so do I.

"Oh!" she cries, putting her hand to her mouth, soothing a cut with her tongue. She exhibits her finger to Paul.

"Really, beauty, it's nothing, just a nick," Paul dismisses. "That didn't even break the skin."

Her next words erupt like lightning:

"God damn you, Paul!" she says. "Is it impossible for you to feel another's fucking pain?"

It is as if she has spewed out a litany of obscenities, the words not hers. She stops soothing her finger; the cut is insignificant. In a soft, almost eerily loving voice, she addresses Paul:

"Is it true, beautiful man, that you detest all women? Is it true that you detest—?"

—me, she doesn't say; the word is suspended.

I walk to her, to be with her when the emotional tempest, the withheld word once spoken—inspired by Elizabeth's prophecy of her imminent ending with Paul—will be set into motion. But the fatal word is blocked. Paul holds her hand and presses it against her mouth. Then he licks the wounded finger, sucking it deep into his mouth, soothing it.

As we stand at the mouth of the stairway, Paul releases her hand and pushes his body against hers; and then holding on to the open bottle of wine, spilling only drops, he lifts her in one swoop and carries her down the stairs.

"Come on, man," he calls, glancing back at me.

I don't move.

"Hey, man!" he urges from downstairs.

31

As I descend to the lowest floor, our desultory laughter recurs, all three of us laughing in spurts as if we've been seeking an evasive object of humor.

In this large room that I have not seen before, the floor is covered with carpeting so soft, so deep that I feel I'm gliding. Through wide windows, blades of moonlight slice the room. A stereo with all its electrical enhancements—Paul has punched buttons on a panel, releasing the sounds—pounds out the violent notes of Bartók's *The Miraculous Mandarin* rushing to its sacrificial ending. He purchased that record for me; I notice next to it Pachelbel's Canon, for Sonya.

Paul lays her on the floor. She stretches, a long, sensual stretch. He sprawls beside her, one of his arms under her head. Her head nestles against him.

"Hey, man," he calls, and nods toward their bodies.

As we do on the sundeck, we'll lie intimately on the carpet to listen to Paul's concert. I move to join them.

I halt.

Paul has removed his trunks—a sudden shock, his nudity while Sonya remains, even if briefly, clothed.

Kneeling over her, he eases off her clothes. She raises her legs to help his movements. She lies naked like an offering. Paul rests on his side next to her, propped slightly toward her. I stare at the two naked bodies. If I add my own to the bared flesh, where will I lie?

The dissonance of Bartók ends, throttled like the mandarin himself.

"Man!" Another invitation from Paul, and a glance up at me. Sonya leans her head back and sideways; her hair tosses in strands over her face—she looks like a gypsy. Paul rolls over her, his legs embracing her body. He kisses her untypically lightly, then harder, hungrily. She responds, eager.

The silence that the violent music has left is replaced by the sound of heat—I *hear* the heat pulsing. Electric air from the fan placed here earlier slices over my body. I shiver, although the night's heat swallows the relief the fan tries to provide.

"Man!"

He wants me to witness his performance, the way he's exhibited his life. I won't be an audience for his sexual prowess. I begin to walk away.

"What the fuck, man?"

I turn back.

He looks up at me, holding me in his gaze, leading it back to him. Then he grasps the open bottle of wine and holds it out to me. Bending, I swig from it, return it to him; he drinks from the bottle. He pours a stream of the wine over Sonya's body. "The best wine, beauty, the very best, almost worthy of your body." His voice is deep, husky, a growled toast, a moan. The liquid flows in a thin streak along her flesh. She shivers. His mouth and tongue—and he looks at me fleetingly to ascertain that I'm watching—follow the jagged course of the wine, over her breasts, her stomach, her thighs. His motions quicken, he slides up to her breasts. A film of oil from the earlier sunning tints their bodies. His tongue glides from one breast to the other. He holds each like an offering. His tongue draws circles around one, slips to the other. The circles narrow on her nipples. He bites them—she winces, then sighs. He keeps the lush flesh in his mouth. He whispers growling words—they sound dirty—into her ears, and he glances up at me. She responds to his words, a low sensual whisper as she dabs at his ear with her tongue.

He takes another swallow of the wine—and I wonder whether it's retained the taste of mine—and from his mouth he drips it between her bronzed legs. His tongue probes and licks there.

I haven't moved.

Her breasts, moistened by the wine and Paul's tongue, are sculpted by the moonlight that darkens behind shreds of clouds, then resurges, brighter.

Sonya's hands roam over Paul's flesh. It gleams with amber moisture. Dots of liquid shine within drifting light. Her hands on his chest coax him back. She bends over him, kissing his chest, gliding over the film of light hairs, lingering with her tongue on his nipples, slipping down to his hardened cock, sucking its head into her mouth, sucking it deeper. She leans back, her body laid out in full display in a glare of light. Tossing, twisting, switching over, back, over, around, up, down, lips pasted, the two bodies morph into one

Paul pushes her back. His cock slides along her wine-tinged body and down to its opening, not entering. She raises herself, urging to be entered. He whispers more words from deep in his throat.

The small triangle between Sonya's legs is so much lighter
than the rest of her darkened body that the difference renders her
even more naked. The flesh about Paul's groin and buttocks—as
his body writhes in shafts of light—is as startling a contrast with
the dark brown of his chest, his legs. As he arches his body over
her, I see his large engorged cock about to enter her. He looks
back at me, smiling a strange smile I can't interpret.

My cock throbs against my trunks. I remove them. I kneel,
closer to the entangled bodies, closer to his body, closer to hers,
close to—I feel the heat of Sonya's flesh, feel the heat of Paul's.
I'm intoxicated by the smell of spilled wine, sweetened sweat,
the sweet rancidity of heated lust. I've achieved a sense that
springs from heated intimacy when—as in drinking together
but not being drunk—there's a stark lucidity that shoves reality
away, becomes reality, and with that comes a sense of terrible
unity in the same overwhelming current, and—alert—I know
we're all flowing in the same clashing tides of blinded lucidity
and false reality.

I lean over the bodies.

Paul is holding Sonya sideways and—

"Taste it, man!"

—toward me, close. He's clasping one of her breasts and—

"Go on, man!"

—giving it to me. A sweetness startles my mouth. I'm
licking her breast, licking the dregs of drying wine, the taste
of his saliva. The rich flesh presses against my mouth. I savor
it, the wine, the flesh, the—

"Yeah!" He smiles the distorted smile.

My head pulls away from Sonya's breast.

Paul straddles her shoulders. His cock over her mouth, her
tongue darts out, moistening its full length, around its thickness,

preparing it. In a violent thrust, he penetrates her. Her body
quivers. He presses in, more, seeking a deeper depth with each
push, pulling out, then lunging in deeper. His hands press her
shoulders down. Her lips part as if to draw his to hers. He
pulls out of her and aims his cock at her face. He slaps her lips
with his cock, he slaps her mouth, slaps across her face, hard,
harder, faster. He is grasping his cock with one hand, and the
harsh sound of slapping comes more from his hand than the
cock it's holding. She tries to wrench her head away. The hard
slapping of his cock and his clenched hand strike harder. Her
head, held down by one of his hands, tries to pull away.

*All charade, acts performed many times before, embellished each
time, a play of control and submission, nothing more, nothing else,
allowed by both, angered dirty commands and threats permitted, intimations of violence permitted, Paul's game of rampant lust . . .* I shake
my head to clear steady confusions. No, it's Paul's voice that
jarred me into the present, his low, guttural demand—

"What the fuck, man?"

—ruptured by words, shouted at Sonya between calls to me:

"Fucken whore . . . you want it in your whore cunt? . . . *Hey,
man!* . . . One cock's not enough for you, bitch? . . . *Man!* . . . You
want two cocks in you, don't you, bitch, don't you?"

It's real, the rage, the angry need, the detestation.

She mutters, sounds.

He smothers her words. "Take it all the way down, you
fucken whore! Keep it in your fucken throat—" His voice is
a growl, a groan, a voice I haven't heard before, the dangerous
voice of a wild animal in heat.

He shoves his pulsing cock into her mouth. She gasps,
gags. Her head attempts to jerk away. His hands press down on
her shoulders. Her hands on his chest push—attempt to push—

—pretend to push him away—

Her nails slide over his flesh. He utters a sound like laughter as she makes a choking sound.

"Choke, fucken cunt, keep it in your fucken throat, bitch, keep it there, and you'll get two."

Jerking her head back forcefully, she says, "Bastard, bastard!"

"Man, come on, man!" Paul looks up at me with a mean, cruel, maddened smile. He pushes her off him. "Kneel, bitch!"

"No!"

"Kneel! Beg! Beg for my cock!"

"Fuck me!"

"Say it louder!"

"Fuck me! Bastard, bastard!"

He pushes her back, mounts her, opens her legs wide, enters her in a lunge, pulls out, then in deeper.

She squirms under him. "Goddamned bastard!"

"This'll shut you up." He raises one hand, over her face, his fingers clench. She twists away from the menacing fist about to come down.

"*Paul!*" I shout—

—and the fist holds midway down, threatening, and he's looking at me, smiling, mouth twisted, smiling—

His fist tenses over her, tightening.

I reach for his arm and hold it. It struggles against my grasp. I clasp it with both hands. The fist begins to unclench, unclenches. I release his hand and it falls to his side. His mouth opens into a roar, laughter that seems to come from beyond him. It stops, choked in his throat, and he smiles the distorted smile.

Straining inside her, owning her, he shouts at her. "Tell me how it feels, whore-bitch. Tell me how it feels. Tell me! *Tell me how it feels!*" The distorted face turns toward me. "You scared of

the cunt? The bitch wants more, man"—pumping into her—
"you scared, you scared?—give her what she wants, man—"

I'm engulfed in a wave of heat, outside and inside, within
a current of hot darkness. I see light-slashed silhouettes of
naked bodies, naked struggling beautiful bodies. I feel a fierce
sexual yearning tinged with meanness and something unrecognized. I stand over naked flesh, breasts, legs, hands, lips,
cunt, cock.

Paul forces her body over him, his cock in her. He shouts
at me: "What ya waitin for, man?"

Desire implodes. I'm reeling in a tide of rage and desire
and rage and lustful urgency as the man pushes the woman
up and down on his cock and his voice spews its litany of
detestation.

"Cock-hungry whore, cunt, tell me how it feels. How
does it feel? You want two cocks?"

I watch bodies soaked with oil and sweat and the glaze
of dried wine, naked straining limbs, straining muscles offered
up to the heat to be devoured by the dark night.

The man's face is the face of a demon, and he is challenging me and laughing and I stare at him and our eyes interlock
and I break the stare and look at the woman's bare skin, dark
velvet, her face a mask of passionate rage.

His cock batters faster. "Come on, man, we'll fuck her
together, man, two cocks in the bitch's cunt." The man's hands
part the woman's buttocks, and he shouts at me:

"Fuck her in the ass, my cock in her cunt—yeah!—fucken
bitch in heat, both cocks in her, man, both cocks, tearing her
cunt, splitting her ass!"

I fling myself over the woman's body that strains over
the man's. My cock slides on oil and sweat, trying to locate

the crack between the woman's buttocks. I raise my hips over her, to lunge. I see the man's contorted sweat-drenched face.

"Fuck her like a dog!"

I arch my body.

"Fuck her like you fuck a man!"

The woman spews an angry sound.

My cock slips over the woman's buttocks.

My face presses against hers, my tongue searches for her lips, my mouth probes hers to open it, to bite her lips, to taste blood.

Moisture—

The moisture of wine—

The moisture of sweat—

The moisture of—

Tears!

The woman's tears—

Sonya's tears!

"Sonya!" I cry and stand up.

She pulls herself away. Paul lies on the floor. Kneeling, Sonya slaps at his face. "Bastard, fucking bastard!"—she slaps at his body— "fucking bastard, bastard!"—and she bends over him, pushing at his body, shoving him over with the strength of her rage, another slide, quickly, quickly, his face down, his legs open. He lies still.

"Fuck him!" she shouts at me. "Fuck him like a dog!"

Then Paul whimpered: "Fuck me."

32

I stepped into the boathouse and released the rowboat. I pushed it onto the lake. I grasped the oars. I was on the lake, letting the boat drift, rowing, drifting on the dark water, rowing, drifting, drifting. . . .

Awake, I was standing. The boat had reached the edge of the moribund island. Purple dawn was descending.

With my eyes closed, I faced the deserted island, preparing for what I knew I would see up close: tangles of shadows, gnarled knots of darkness, the ashen debris of a long-smoldering fire that might seem still to attempt to flare out of decay, a house gutted by flames, walls crumpled into a mound of rotting debris.

I opened my eyes.

In the blue mist of twilight melting into the brightness of the new day, there it stood: the large house intact, the surrounding grounds unviolated. As if the conspiracy of darkness and shadows I had witnessed never existed.

But it had, must have.

I rowed around the island, to the back.

There it was, what I had seen, the devastation, an ashen crumbling cave carved out of the large house by fire that had ravaged only this side of the island. It was all here—only here—ripped shreds of wood, mutilated pieces of what once was, the jetsam of catastrophe.

I rowed away.

I tied up the rowboat in its place. As I ran to my room, silence battered my ears. I threw myself into bed and longed for sleep.

I woke and remembered footsteps, someone entering my room and fleeing when I stirred. I stumbled back into sleep, and woke again as if I was being yanked out of a deep dark depth—and I saw it propped against the typewriter on the desk, a book. I got up. I read the book's title:

The Origin of Evil
by
V. K. Edelstein

I lifted it, ominously heavy, and set it flat before me on the table. Inserted within its pages was an old newspaper or magazine article—difficult to tell which, since it was old, though preserved, cut out, and carefully folded—and there was with it a yellow sheet on which were scribbled words. The sheet had been crumpled as if discarded but pressed back and restored. The footsteps I had heard—they belonged to whoever had brought this book and its inserts to me; I did not remember the inserts when I first encountered the book in the library.

I opened its first pages and read:

Foreword

The matter of evil, most often referred to as "the problem of evil," has been a subject explored throughout time. Every religion has examined it. Philosophers have added volumes. Authors and poets have dramatized it. All have claimed to have found an answer. Some have claimed the answer.

It is not my intention to deal with the beliefs advanced by established religious or philosophical doctrines. Those are widely recorded and analyzed.

In this book, I shall delve only into theories rejected by establishmentarians, beliefs dismissed as derived by cults, invented and perpetuated as myths, shunned as superstition—often as the work of the Devil himself. A main determination in my choices for exploration is that they have spawned notable followings and disciples, adherents that prevail.

I opened the book. The placement of the inserted article signaled this page for attention. I read:

Professor Emanuel Elgard of Hamburg University is the proponent of the theory of the Indomitability and Endurability of Evil, a theory that became widely popular at the inception of the twentieth century. Subsequently it has predominated as the dogma of a secret society with many devoted adherents. In dealing with Dr. Elgard's ideology, or theology as its disciples claim, I shall only quote in order to preserve the tone of the author's presentation, since even devotees of his philosophy consider it at times arcane, elevated in language, elements they claim are intentional, including its flights of verbiage.

In approaching his beliefs thus, I will ensure accuracy.

I now venture into Dr. Elgard's philosophy:

"What happens to Evil when Its flames are snuffed? Does It hide? Does It wait to spring out again? Like matter, Evil can be neither created nor destroyed. It is an entity. It exists in perpetuity. It was and is and will be. It remains festering in the soil of great violence."

Those words—I had read them. No, I had heard them. Paul had uttered something like that when we arrived at the edge of his island. He had spoken—quoted—them as he stared toward the vacated island. He had laughed the words away, deriding them as "lofty shit."

I pushed the book back. I was in no mood—a headache was pulsating at my temples—to read any more. I have always disdained mysticism, including its esoteric language, although in college I admired the brooding of the sixteenth-century metaphysical poets.

Heat had not abated. Sweat was running down my body. I staggered to the shower. Only when the cold water drenched my flesh did I realize I had remained undressed since last night. Last night . . . contorted bodies tossing.

I dried myself. I put on the army fatigues I had brought. As if it was pulling me back, I returned to the book. I read where I had left off:

Alerted about other fertile soil, the seeds of violence already planted, *and invited to invade, as the Daemon summons His willing victims . . .*

I halted, jolted by the aroused association: ". . . willing victims." That resonating phrase had become hateful to me since Paul had connected it to me. Did he really believe its implication that it granted him license for cruelty? I needed to disbelieve that. I needed to believe that his advocacy of that implication was a prop for his self-vaunted image as indomitable.

More words from the enraged book:

Evil prepares to sweep forth to new territory, Its new awaiting destination, moving ever closer like an Omen on black clouds that burst into shadows of shadows that exist with no need of light, and It will soar on the wings of the Daemon from Its previous dregs of decay, leaving it abandoned, some might claim cleansed—

My impression of the house on the island had been of catastrophic darkness, but only earlier a flood of new light had cleansed that view. Confusion was easily explained: I had viewed the distant island from several vantages and altered light. . . . I had to stop imposing meaning on this esoteric verbiage.

I read more:

Resistance to Evil violates man's nature, once he has perceived Its beckoning. To deny Its power, to interfere with Its ineluctable progression, is not possible. It is to be accepted and welcomed and joined. . . .

The quagmire of prose, wandering phrases, repetition—all spoke of a hallucinating, sick mind, the terrifying raging of a madman. How was it ever taken seriously?

I felt dizzy, as if I was trapped within the zigzagging colors and lines of the painting over the desk—I had just looked up at it; the towel I covered it with last night had fallen. Last night ... angry flesh, beautiful angry flesh. ...

I flipped through more pages, grasping a word here, a phrase there: "the miasma of rot ... waves of roaring silence advancing ... the flowering of evil seeds ... mournful flowers of sweet decay ... flowing from the site of devouring fire ..."

I pushed the book away decisively. But its words festered: "... fertile soil, seeds of violence planted ..." I closed my eyes, rejecting the overpowering urge to force connections with this hysterical foreboding.

I would leave it exactly as I found it, signaling to whoever had placed it here that I had ignored it. A stupid prank! Stanty! Goddamn that son of a bitch, his fucken prank. He saw me in the library looking for that crazy fucken book. ...

Urgent coded information ...

The effects of last night, the heat, the liquor ... naked bodies glowing with oil, knifed into white gleaming slashes by the moon.

"Seeds of evil planted ... fertile soil ... a new awaiting destination ..." Just the ridiculous spewing of an insane mind.

I needed to leave this room, go outside; yes, and all would be as it had been, just like other times.

"Incipient Evil waiting to erupt within the sultry heat ..."

Perspiration coated my skin like a sheet of steam.

I glance once at the book I had closed. It lies there, dark, commanding, radiating its message of violence swept forth within dark clouds shattering into black shadows of shadows without light. ... The murmuring undercurrent I had once detected.

Absurd. I was tired, reeling from last night's liquor. I had allowed my own fevered mind to range. My head was clearing.

I felt like laughing at myself for the seriousness with which I had been responding to this raging madman Elgard.

With a sense of frustrated resignation that I should feel compelled to continue to attend to this cache of strange information, and despite fearing that what I would uncover might compound rather than clarify new questions, I reached for the printed article, and—noticing immediately that dates and location had been inked over, rendering the account timeless—I read:

33

Catastrophe on Island Remembered
Two Survivors Still Missing

After ███ years, mystery and rumors still surround the fiery catastrophe that erupted on a private island on an unnamed lake outside the village of ███████████. The only two survivors, an unidentified young man and a young woman, remain unaccounted for despite repeated attempts to locate them. The debacle claimed the lives of all twelve guests—including, it has been claimed without authentication, defrocked Cardinal ████████████████████, missing since the notorious scandal involving █████████████ of ████████████ and the ████████████ from ████████████ sent him into undisclosed exile. Unverified accounts, all that remain, assert that he was the secret owner of the island bought under a false name. Whether the fire burst out in a natural way or was set by someone on the island is unknown at the

time this account is being written on the supposed
anniversary of the tragedy.

The fire ravaged a section of the house where all the
guests convened, entrapping them. Some broke out by shattering windows and tried futilely to reach the lake. "Fire
must have spread with the speed of a demonic creature,"
according to Captain ███████ ██████████ (now
deceased), the first official responder to the fire. Access
was impeded by the location on the lake and by the
attempted and blocked influx of the curious rowing to
the island alerted by flames seen miles away.

Despite the ensuing chaos and futile attempts
by firefighters to reach the conflagration, Captain
████████████ was able briefly to question the two
young witnesses apparently employed on the island and
therefore quartered in a part of the house left astonish-
ingly unaffected by the fire.

In his hurried report of his encounter with the
two survivors, Captain ████████████ maintained that
"the boy and the girl appeared surprisingly composed
though on reflection they were in a state of shock, staring down blankly. The only explanation for the fire the
girl was able to convey, in words I wrote immediately
and exactly lest I forget, was that 'gray fog thick as smoke
would not lift, heating the shadows.' The boy added his
own babbled words, declaring that 'it was the heat of the
dark clouds that turned into flames as if the lake was on
fire and burning smoke was racing away.'" The fact that
Captain ███████████ was himself in shock may explain
his confused recollection, which some have questioned.

Attempts to locate the two witnesses after ██ years have been as unsuccessful as have the attempts to verify the names of the reputedly wealthy guests, although from time to time a guarded name surfaces. It has been conjectured that any investigation has been thwarted by powerful persons in high places in order to avoid an even greater scandal.

The Great Fire on the Lake, as it is now designated, has remained as mysterious as on the day it burst into tragedy.

Gossip persists that before the fire, rituals and practices among the selected guests were violent and vile, "unholy rituals."

34

Unwanted images battered my mind. I had seen both the untouched portion of the house and the spectacle of the decaying island. I pushed away the account of the fire. I could dismiss it easily. Its ominous intimations were the product of a clumsy village reporter pumping up his report with sensationalized conclusions.

But Elgard's words from his theory of evil persisted.

"Thick fog . . . bursting shadows . . . unabating heat . . ."

I felt cold in the heat. My head was reeling. I reached for the yellow sheet of paper scrawled with handwritten notes. The sheet was crumpled, discarded, retrieved, and restored—by the writer or someone else. I recognized Paul's handwriting from his letters. I read:

> to study him   to see myself becoming as I was
> becoming what I am   to ward him away or toward
> whichever is revealed   by him   by me away or
> from that goal   the trap beautiful or harrowing to
> be found   a search for him   searched myself
> and found demonic angels   I study my beloved
> son, my Stanty, my Constantine   to find myself

becoming   reasons   motives   What one
became, what the other will become ...

I looked up from the puzzling words. Demonic angels—
my phrase; at least some of the notes were written during our
association. They seemed to echo equally disjointed words
Paul had uttered when I questioned his view of Stanty. A
struggle to understand himself, "becoming"?—a confrontation with himself? These notes—written for whom? to me?
as an attempted answer to my question?—written and then
discarded. Left by whom along with the fraudulent book?
And why?

I read the last lines, the clearest entry, as if through the
desultory thoughts Paul had drawn a possible conclusion.

Him, my son, my beloved son, my Constantine—
release him? Shall I free him? Can I free him? Is it
too late, the infernal trap sprung?

Free him? Did he mean finally to separate Stanty from
him, how he saw himself and Stanty, "becoming"? If that were
possible—considering Stanty's capacity for violence that I had
experienced—would Stanty let *him*, Paul, go? Free *Paul*?

Then the fleeting clarity I had grasped vanished. Through
all those revelations about himself—and these tortured
thoughts—would Paul be forever an enigma?

I restored his notes as I remembered finding them within
the book, which I propped up as I had found it. Then I withdrew the yellow sheet with the notes. I folded that sheet and
secured it in the drawer among my clothes to keep.

My head was clear. Now, to fulfill what I saw as the stern direction of this fading day, I had to resurrect in my mind the events of last night.

I see Paul on the floor. I see Sonya's fists flailing at him. "Fuck him!" I hear her say, "Fuck him like a dog!"—and I heard Paul whimper: "Fuck me." I throw myself over him, my body pressed against his drenched in sweat and oil. My cock begins to enter, only the tip—no, my whole body pushes—entering. He twists, uttering a sound like a moan of pain or pleasure, pain and pleasure. I push in more, harder. He winces and a moan slides into a sigh, back to a low moan. I wait, and then I thrust in and out, remain deep in, cherishing the ecstasy of this invasion that fuses our bodies into one. Spurting eruptions of my cum glue us together, his body contracts, he gasps, and still inside him, I can feel the throbbing of his cock, I feel his eruption in spurts. I pull out of him, drops of my cum spill on him. I run out past Sonya. She stands staring down at Paul.

35

Night had come over me with such insistence that I did not realize till now that I had escaped into sleep. A startling coolness had wakened me, and with it the awareness that—impossible, so soon?—this was the time of ending, the beginning of summer's end. Only days ago, Paul had informed me of the approaching date of his departure. "You can stay here until before winter if you want," he told me. "This is a good place to write. In winter it's uninhabitable—the water freezes over." I glanced about the room I would be leaving.

The strange book was gone—and, with it, the account of the island atrocity. I got up to search for the yellow sheet, Paul's intimate notes. It was where I had hidden it. I would keep those notes.

A soft knock at the door. I slipped on my army fatigues.

Sonya came into my room. A mixture of pleasure and apprehension alerted me that this was the first time I had seen her since the infinite distance from last night.

She sat on the bed, next to me.

"I came to say—"

"No," I interrupted. I had to speak first. "About what

happened—" I was about to say I was sorry, but that was inade-
quate. I shifted: "I didn't stop what was happening because I
thought Paul was playing one of his games until it turned ugly
and then I did stop it—please remember that, Sonya. I stopped
it when"—I couldn't say the words *when he threatened to strike
you.* "I was a coward, but I did stop it."

"Shhhh," she said. She touched my lips with one finger,
holding it there, removed it. "It was all a game."

"You're lying."

She jerked away from me. "We played a game, John," she
said, facing me.

"But you were crying, I felt your tears."

"Those were *your* tears." She did not look away from me.

She was lying, I knew it, I had to know it, and I had to
force her away from those deadly lies: "Paul wasn't playing
when he clenched his fist to—"

She raised her voice. "Goddammit, John, Paul would never
hit me!" She stood up, rigid before me.

"Sonya—"

"It was a game, goddammit—*and we all played it!*"

I stood before her. Only silence was possible for this infin-
ity of moments.

Her voice relented: "I came to tell you that I'm returning
to Paris with Paul."

"You're staying with him?"

"Of course. I love him," she said as if that was the only
answer. "I'm leaving now, the boat and the car are waiting."

Today—leaving today?

"Paul is staying only to take care of some business with
the village attorney. I'm meeting him in New York. We're fly-
ing together."

Her words sounded rehearsed, weary—or perhaps I only wanted to believe that and nothing more, nothing else she was saying, nothing she had said.

Her expression softened. She seemed about to touch me. She turned and moved away. She paused at the door. She faced me.

"Good-bye . . . my dear John."

Would I ever, ever believe her? "Good-bye . . . Sonya."

Appearing in my room abruptly as he always did, for surprise, Stanty stood at attention before me; he was wearing a vaguely military uniform. Before I could demand that he get the fuck out—

"I came to say good-bye, John Rechy," he said, with a slight bow. "My father is driving me to school today."

I did not move.

"Good-bye . . . John Rechy," he repeated, almost in a whisper. He held out his hand to me.

I stared at him in disgusted fascination. Did he really believe that I would touch him—touch the hand that would have lunged out of the black water and pulled me down?

My hand extends.

He takes it. His hand is cold, bloodless.

I try to pull my hand away. He clasps it.

I yank away from the deadened flesh.

Paul stood with me on the lawn, awaiting word that the car that would take him to the airport had arrived. He had just completed his business in the village. I had not seen him—I had been avoiding him—since the drunken, feverish night.

"Have you considered staying longer, to write?" he asked me.

"Maybe. Briefly."

He gave me instructions on how the house would be closed.

We walked toward the boat.

"Where will you go from here?" Paul asked me.

"A big city." I looked across the lawn, where I had first seen the somber dark statues.

Paul took another step toward the motorboat. He turned to look at me and then walked back. "John—"

What had occurred among Sonya, him, and me, that drunken feverish night, had been left unspoken. He would speak about it now.

"John—" Again, only my name.

"Paul—"

He moved close to me, so close that I thought I could hear his heart beating—or mine. He embraced me, tightly. He kissed me on the mouth, his tongue darted about my lips to open them. My lips remained closed. When his retreated, I touched my mouth. There was no trace of blood on my finger.

"Good-bye . . . Paul."

"Man? . . . Good-bye."

36

I was alone on the island.

I returned to the room where, that sweaty night, Paul and I and Sonya—

Sonya . . .

I listened to the Bartók music that had played that night, music whose contortions had melded with spiraling dark heat.

l returned to my room.

That night alone on the island—I had not seen the gray couple since they had taken Paul to the mainland—I welcomed the lingering coolness from the open window. I slid into sleep.

I was wakened by a thrust of heat. My sweat had soaked the sheet into an outline of my body. I got up; it was still night; I went outside, hoping for a breeze; the heat followed, unrelenting. A pallid moon was retreating under a gray smear of clouds. I did what I had avoided the last few days. I looked toward the neighboring island. As the feeble reflection of the moon struggled out of the lake, I saw it. A heavy black shawl of clouds was floating from it, abandoning the neighboring island and floating over the lake. Under the drowning light, shadows swerved about the edges of this island.

I returned inside the house.

In my room, deep darkness gathered at the window, attempting to enter—an impression so powerful that I pulled back until with vast relief I realized I had dropped into sleep, lulled by the murmurs from the lake and by a sense of wearied resignation about the resurgence of heat.

I woke up startled by a sound like a smothered roar, a silent roar, fading loudly. I forced my concentration onto the restless swooshing of the rowboats against the house. Roiling waves of darkness quivered at the window, pushing in, swarming into the room, invading the house—I had left my room to verify that—heated night bursting through the windows, the doors, the crevices, flooding the island with flames of darkness.

In the morning, when the distorted shadows I had imagined invading the house—I was sure I had imagined them—had been banished by the glare of the sun, I packed my duffel bag.

I did not have to call the gray couple. Perhaps alerted by noise in my room and now by my footsteps, they appeared in the hall, waiting. My duffel bag rested beside me on the floor. The man approached, to lift it for me. I reached down to take it myself. I reared back. I saw his hand on the looped strap of my duffel bag. Fire had scorched his skin, which, long-healed, had assumed a scarred, crinkled whiteness. Sensing my stare, he straightened up but did not hide his hand. The woman glided beside him. Their eyes lifted and met my stare.

With unbudging certainty, I knew then who they were. In acknowledgement of that powerful discovery, I nodded.

They answered my nod, the slightest movement.

The man grabbed my duffel bag. We walked to the dock, where the motorboat waited. He put my duffel bag in the boat.

The woman arranged it there. Both as silent as they had always been, their eyes downcast again, they started the motorboat.

Before I entered it, I gazed at the neighboring island. It was purified of all the rot, abandoned by the clouds, which—

—were lunging to invade this island with shadows so black—those words were etched into my mind—that they did not need the source of light.

The couple took me to the shoreline, where the car they had summoned waited.

Without facing back, I whispered, "Island . . . island," the words fading even as I spoke them.

Then I left.